Delighting Mrs. Bennet

Delighting Mrs. Bennet

A Pride and Prejudice Variation

LEENIE BROWN

LEENIE B BOOKS

HALIFAX

Contents

Dear Reader,

Once upon a time...well, actually, a couple of years ago, I began a weekly writing exercise on my blog (leeniebrown.com) and called it Thursday's Three Hundred. What was supposed to be just a few minutes of practice – just three hundred words a week – quickly took on a life of its own and became something much grander.

To date, those writing exercises have produced one short story (*Hope at Dawn*), a four-book series (*Willow Hall Romance*), a stand-alone novella (*With the Colonel's Help*), the first book in this series (*Confounding Caroline*) and now, this novel that you hold in your hand.

While some things about how I create these stories have evolved since that first writing exercise, the tradition of posting a portion of a work in progress continues each Thursday. In fact, there is a new story posting there now.

Chapter 1

"How is he?" Darcy stopped pacing the sitting room as his physician, Mr. Westcott, entered.

"I have seen worse." He cast a glance at the others in the room but spoke to Darcy. "Mr. Royston had some difficulty setting the bone. I would not move him for at least two weeks."

"He may stay where he is, of course," Darcy assured Mr. Westcott.

"I suspected you would say that." Mr. Westcott turned his hat in his hand and smiled at Darcy. "I have left instructions for Mr. Bennet's care with Mr. Abrams, and he informed me that he would find someone to assign to my patient."

He reached down and scratched the head of the black and tan dog standing at his side. "A fine mess you made, lad," he chided.

The dog cocked his head to the side and seemed

to smile, utterly unaware of the damage his racing about in a frenzy of fun had caused.

"Stick to chasing rats," Mr. Westcott added with a pat for the happy beast's head.

"I have never had a pup that was so difficult to train," Darcy apologized. He snapped his fingers at the dog and was completely ignored. Every other dog which had come into Darcy's possession had learned to stop and look when they heard his snap, but not Dash.

Dash was his own dog. It was not that he was incapable of learning commands. No, he was an intelligent beast, wily even, and adept at finding all kinds of mischief into which to toss himself with abandon. He was just unwilling to follow a command unless he determined first that it should be followed.

"Strength of character is not so bad a thing." Mr. Westcott patted Dash's head again. "It is a great asset once it has been properly directed."

Darcy sighed. "That is the struggle." He looked at Dash and made a clucking sound while tapping his leg.

Dash tipped his head so that one ear flopped up as he looked at Darcy and paused for a moment before deciding that standing at Darcy's side would be the thing to do. And he almost made it to Darcy's side before being distracted by a pair of pretty slippers.

"He'll come around," Mr. Westcott assured Darcy. "He's young."

Elizabeth pulled her feet under her chair and, bending forward, scratched Dash's ear while he looked from her hidden slippers to her face and back.

"Our patient is well-settled?" Mr. Westcott asked Mr. Royston as he entered the room.

"He is, sir. He will likely sleep for some time."

"At present, the more sleeping he does, the better," Mr. Westcott said. "I shall return tomorrow, but if anything changes, you know where you can find me."

"Two weeks," Elizabeth said to Dash as Darcy walked to the door of the sitting room with Mr. Westcott and his assistant. "My father must stay in bed for two weeks, and who knows how long after that it will be before he is walking properly." She leveled a severe look at the animal which was happily accepting her attention. "You were a very naughty pup," she chided.

Dash ducked his head and looked up at her with sad eyes.

"Do not think I will fall for that," Elizabeth said with a chuckle. "You are still a naughty pup."

"Perhaps if you did not scratch his ear while reprimanding him, it might have a greater effect," said Mrs. Gardiner.

Elizabeth sighed. "I cannot help it. His ears just beg to be scratched, and if I do not scratch them, he will attempt to chew my slipper with my foot still in it."

"I should send him to John at Pemberley," Darcy said from the doorway to the drawing room. "John always knows how to get an animal to mind." He shook his head. "Of course, Georgiana would be sorely displeased if I did. However, I do believe he will be confined to Georgiana's sitting room when we have guests take a tour of the house."

He blew out a breath and crossed the room to sit with the ladies. "I must apologize for the damage Dash has caused. There are no words for how dreadful I feel." How did one make amends for his dog tripping a gentleman and causing him to tumble down the stairs, resulting in a broken leg?

"It is not as if you expected it to happen," Mrs. Gardiner said.

"But if he were better trained..." He stopped his protest at the lift of the lady's brow and the incredulous look she gave him.

"Babies, which Dash is, do not always mind their parent. Trust me. I know. I have four children, Mr. Darcy, and there are days I wonder whose offspring they are, for surely my children would not behave in such an inappropriate fashion." She sighed. "But alas, they are mine. However, each possesses his or her own temperament and will. And Dash, I would imagine, is not so very different." She smiled. "I find biscuits work quite well to encourage proper behaviour."

Darcy chuckled. "Dash does enjoy biscuits."

A footman, carrying a leash, came into the room, and immediately, Dash scooted between Elizabeth's chair and the wall.

Darcy took a small piece of cake from the tea tray, which had yet to be removed from the room after the commotion of a falling father and the doctor being summoned. Crouching down, he extended it to Dash. The cake proved to be far too tempting for Dash to ignore, and soon, the footman was leaving the room with Dash trotting happily behind him while Darcy returned to his chair and the room fell silent.

"I should like to look in on my father before we go, even if he is sleeping," Elizabeth said.

"Of course," Darcy agreed. "Is there any way you might be able to stay with him?" Darcy knew it was unlikely, but he also knew that Elizabeth would wish to see to her father's care. From the hopeful look Elizabeth shared with her aunt, he knew he was correct.

"I fear there is not," Mrs. Gardiner answered.

Darcy nodded and again the room fell into silence, save for the ticking of the clock on the table in the corner. In Darcy's mind, it was not right that a man should be without at least someone from his family near him when he was convalescing. The someone should be Elizabeth. She would, no doubt, know best how to cheer her father and keep him entertained. However, without some sort of able-bodied chaperone to ensure that things were kept proper, it was not possible for her to attend to her father without risking damage to her reputation. His brows furrowed as he considered asking his aunt to come for a visit, but the countess was a stranger to Elizabeth, and that would not do. Perhaps...

"What if your mother were to come to town?" Darcy asked.

"My mother?" Elizabeth's eyes were wide.

Darcy nodded. "Yes, your mother. Then you and your sister could stay here, and your father would not be alone."

Elizabeth shook her head, her look clearly telling him that she thought he was not thinking clearly. "My mother will bring all of my sisters."

"I know," Darcy admitted, "but I thought you might wish to care for your father, and I cannot think of any other way to make it possible."

"I would be delighted to care for him," Elizabeth replied, "but my mother?" She turned to her sister. "Jane, tell him he does not want our mother here. In town. At his house."

"It is only two weeks," Darcy argued. "I am certain I could perform the part of host admirably for two weeks." He was almost certain that was true. Surely, two weeks would be endurable.

Elizabeth sent a pleading look to her sister.

"Our mother is trying," Jane said. "Darcy House is so peaceful," she grimaced, "but it would not be after the arrival of our mother." She paused. "And sisters."

Darcy knew Jane was correct, but he was determined to do what he thought was his duty.

"No," he said, shaking his head, "I am inviting your mother and sisters to Darcy House." His stomach twisted at the thought. The more he thought about it, the more he did not know how he would tolerate so much noise in his home, but it had to be done. His dog had caused Mr. Bennet's injury, and Darcy would bear the discomfort of Mrs. Bennet's presence in return.

Chapter 2

Darcy rubbed the back of his neck and reclined in his chair as he studied the letter before him. As much as he had insisted – multiple times – to Elizabeth, Jane, and Mrs. Gardiner that he was capable of tolerating Mrs. Bennet, and as much as he attempted to assure himself that it was true, he was not entirely certain that he had not overestimated his ability to abide so many people in his private domain. He scowled at the dog lying in front of the hearth.

"You look rather displeased," Colonel Richard Fitzwilliam said as he entered Darcy's study.

"Do you ever wait to be announced?"

Richard shrugged out of his coat and unbuttoned his waistcoat. "I do not need an introduction. You know me. We are family, and as Aunt Catherine always says, there is no need to tell my family who I am." He smirked as he tossed both his jacket and his waistcoat onto a chair and crossed to where Darcy kept a decanter of port and glasses.

"You may be known to me, but there are times I would like a few fleeting seconds to gather my thoughts before they are intruded upon." He nodded as Richard lifted a glass in offer.

"So tell me," Richard said as he poured, ignoring Darcy's reprimand, as he often did. "What has you scowling at poor little Dash."

"Naughty little Dash," Darcy corrected. "I have a houseguest for the next two weeks, at least, and I was just writing to invite four more guests to join us, all thanks to that naughty little pup."

The fashion in which his cousin slowly sat the decanter down and methodically turned toward Darcy as if he expected to see something hideous or to be faced with the barrel of a pistol caused Darcy to smile, despite his displeasure with Dash and his misgivings about the invitation which lay on his desk.

"I assure you I have not lost my mind."

Richard lifted a brow. "You just admitted to inviting five people to stay with you. That is not something you do."

Darcy blew out a breath and began folding his letter. "I have no choice, and it might actually be more than five people."

"First, you decide to marry, and now, you are filling your house with guests. Should the home office hear of this, they might rightly send a couple men to ensure you have not been kidnapped and replaced by an imposter." He chuckled as he placed a glass on the desk in front of Darcy.

"Now, just a moment, young pup," he scolded as he saw Dash leap into the chair on which Richard had tossed his clothing and begin to circle before lying down. "My clothes are not your bed." Richard shooed the beast onto the floor.

"I told you. He is a wayward pup. Nearly incorrigible."

Richard bent and scratched the dog's ears. "He merely wants more instruction."

"Why must everyone give him attention when he misbehaves?" It was as if those ears had some sort of magical pull on everyone who came near them.

"He is doing as he is supposed to at present. My jacket is safe; therefore, he deserves a scratch."

Darcy shook his head. "Your jacket is only safe until you turn your back."

To prove his point, Darcy said nothing when Dash once again sprang onto the chair and made a bed of his cousin's jacket, but he did chuckle when, this time, Richard added a curse to his command to get off his clothes.

Dash, apparently, knew that he had crossed some line and scooted back to the hearth with his ears flattened and his tail tucked.

"And you had best stay there for a time," Richard said to the animal while settling into the chair he always claimed when he visited Darcy in his study.

Darcy chuckled and finished folding and sealing his letter before he made his way to the study door and requested that it be posted express as soon as possible. He was not in a rush to have Mrs. Bennet and her younger daughters descend upon him, but he was eager to allow Elizabeth the opportunity to care for her father.

"What was that about?" Richard asked as Darcy joined him near the hearth. Dash popped up when Darcy approached, but a gruff word from Richard returned him to his place.

"Dash has decided that I am inviting Mrs. Bennet and her remaining daughters to Darcy House."

Richard cocked his head to the side and drew his eyebrows together until they nearly touched.

"While Mr. Bennet and his family were taking a tour of Darcy House this afternoon, Dash decided to break into one of his racing fits. You know how he gets."

Richard nodded.

"He circled the hall in front of the guest rooms, tore down the stairs, toppled something in the blue drawing room, and on his way back up the stairs, darted under Mr. Bennet's foot."

Darcy nodded in response to Richard's look and gasp of alarm. "Mr. Bennet tumbled. His leg is broken, and he cannot be moved for two weeks."

"Dash can be sold." Richard gave the dog a pointed look.

"Not if we wish to keep Georgiana happy. She is quite attached to him."

"Females and their dashed sensibilities," Richard muttered.

"I'd send him to Pemberley were it not for her, but she is doing so well. I should hate to be the cause of any sorrow for her."

His sister had weathered the devastation of discovering her affections, which had been incited in an attempt to claim her fortune, had not been returned. It had taken her months to begin returning to the happy girl he had always known her to be. Even if she was more serious now than she had been before the ordeal with Wickham in Ramsgate, she was not so grave and despondent as she had been at first.

"So, the pup stays," Richard agreed. "As does Mr. Bennet."

Darcy nodded.

"And you are inviting Mrs. Bennet to care for her husband? I had thought she was a silly woman. Is that not how you described her?"

A great sigh escaped Darcy as he nodded again. "What am I to do? The man needs his family near him, and without a proper chaperone, it cannot be either Miss Bennet or Miss Elizabeth. You know how it would be. Two single young ladies staying with a single gentleman — to whom neither is related but who is courting one of those young ladies while his good friend is betrothed to the other — would cause talk."

A slow smile crept across Richard's face, causing a slow burning to creep up Darcy's neck.

"I will not deny that the idea of having Miss Elizabeth under my roof is not a pleasant one, but I assure you that is not why I wish to have her here. She is her father's favourite. Surely, he will feel most content if she is near."

Richard chuckled and nodded. "As will you." He drained the last bit of port from his glass and then held it out for Dash to lick, ignoring Darcy's protests. "The mother comes with more daughters, does she not?"

"Most likely." Darcy blew out a breath. He dreaded the arrival of the younger Bennets almost more than their mother.

"How will you keep them entertained?"

Darcy shrugged. "I had hoped they would bring their own entertainment." His sister was proficient at keeping herself occupied.

Richard made an uncertain sound of disbelief. "There is also the park and the museum," he suggested. "And do not forget shopping. There is not a female alive that I know of who does not enjoy a trip to the shops."

Darcy groaned. Entertaining the youngest Bennets was definitely going to be trying. But, he thought as he emptied his glass, seeing Elizabeth happy would be worth the discomfort. Or so he hoped.

Chapter 3

"Lizzy," Mrs. Gardiner said softly as her niece rose and paced to the window for the third time in only three times as many minutes.

Elizabeth drew the right corner of her lower lip between her teeth as she turned toward her aunt. How could she not pace and fidget? "Mama will be here soon," she whispered, casting a look toward the bed where her father was sleeping.

"And I am certain all is in order and ready for her arrival." Mrs. Gardiner joined her niece at the window.

Elizabeth shook her head and wrapped her arms around her middle. Having a room ready to receive a guest was not enough preparation for the arrival of her mother.

"Mr. Darcy is not prepared. I know he has said he is, but he is not. Do not look at me like that. I know

I am correct." She blew out a breath and turned back to the window.

Her mother would set Mr. Darcy's well-ordered world on its head, and then? Then, she would once again lose Mr. Darcy's good opinion, and that thought caused her eyes to sting with tears and her heart to beat as rapidly as a horse flying across an open field.

"He will still love you despite your mother or your sisters," Mrs. Gardiner whispered as she placed an arm around Elizabeth's shoulders.

Elizabeth's brow furrowed. Her aunt was very good at figuring out what was truly bothering her, even when Elizabeth did not say a word.

Her aunt pulled her close and added, "Should it appear that Mr. Darcy is struggling to keep his equanimity, you need only send word, and your uncle and I will take your mother to Gracechurch Street." Her head tipped to the side. "Of course, that would mean you must also return to us. You cannot stay here unchaperoned."

Elizabeth expelled a resigned sigh and nodded slowly. The thought of leaving her father did not sit well with her. However, the thought of leaving Darcy House did not seem to disturb her only because it meant leaving her father. She had not even been here for more than a few hours each day, and yet, she had found herself growing oddly attached to her surroundings.

There was a soft rap at the door before it opened, and Mr. Darcy, the likely reason why Elizabeth was growing so attached to Darcy House, stepped into the room. Her lips curled into a smile at the sight of him.

"Is your father sleeping comfortably?" he asked softly once he had crossed to where Elizabeth stood with her aunt.

"He says the pain is not so bad today as it has been," she answered.

"I am glad."

"As are we all," Mrs. Gardiner said.

"Were you watching the street?" Darcy asked with a nod toward the window.

Elizabeth nodded. "She will be here soon."

He extended his arm to her. "That is why I have come. You should be among the first to greet your mother." He turned his head toward Mrs. Gardiner once Elizabeth had placed her hand on his arm. "I have a footman in the hall who will take your place."

"You are very thoughtful," Mrs. Gardiner said with a smile.

Darcy shook his head. "No, I am self-indulgent, for I find myself quite unequal to greeting my guests on my own."

Elizabeth turned worried eyes toward her aunt.

"I am certain you would acquit yourself of the duty perfectly," Mrs. Gardiner said, favouring her anxious niece with a pointed look before she and Jane followed her from the room.

"I am not so confident in my abilities as you are, Mrs. Gardiner," Darcy replied as they reached the hall.

"My mother can join us at Gracechurch Street," Elizabeth offered.

"You are not the only one who is uneasy, Mr. Darcy," Mrs. Gardiner added. "Mrs. Bennet can be a trial at times."

"You are worried?" Darcy asked her.

"Not I so much as Elizabeth," Mrs. Gardiner replied.

"I assure you I am prepared for your mother and sisters to arrive and turn my well-ordered life on its head."

Elizabeth loved the playful smile which accompanied his words — no, they were not his words, they were her words. He was quoting her, after all. How many times had she used that phrase about his well-ordered life when trying to dissuade him from his foolish notion of entertaining not only her injured father but also her mother and sisters?

"Truth be told," he continued with a sheepish grin. "I have made no secret of my desire to one day see you as mistress of this very home."

Elizabeth could feel her cheeks growing warm. The dour and reserved Mr. Darcy from Hertford-shire seemed nearly a thing of the past, for in the days since she had agreed to a courtship when standing in the hall at the Johnson's ball, he had become quite bold in his proclamations regarding their future. The dining room would be the one over which she presided one day. The menu would be hers to approve. The drawing room was no longer his but rather ours. It was nearly too much for her to take in in so short a space of time, but it was not off-putting. She rather liked how he seemed to be claiming her not only as a wife but a partner.

"Therefore," Darcy continued as Elizabeth attempted to keep her thoughts and emotions under regulation, "I thought it only fitting for you to be at my side when your mother arrives." His smile had shifted to something more sly and cunning than sheepish. "And I wish for her to see you at my side. I have been assured that she knows nothing of our courtship, and I find the idea of revealing such a thing in such a way to be oddly tantalizing. I honestly do not know why. It is not my normal wont to taunt and tease. I leave such things to my cousin. However, upon discussing your mother with your father yesterday, I agreed that to alter her view of you could be enjoyable."

Elizabeth's mouth dropped open. Her father, even in his injured state, was still provoking her mother and using Mr. Darcy to do so? Oh, he was incorrigible!

"And Mr. Bingley has arrived to add to the excitement," Darcy added.

"I fear you have lost your mind completely!" Elizabeth declared. "The whole square shall reverberate with her shrieks of delight."

"Or she might just faint away," said Mrs. Gardiner with a chuckle.

"We might want to hope for that," said Jane.

"No," Darcy assured Elizabeth as they reached

the bottom of the stairs. "I have not lost my mind, just my heart."

Elizabeth attempted to scowl at him but could not. She was not made of stone. So, instead, she just shook her head while she smiled that foolish smile she seemed to wear whenever he said anything about loving her. It was utterly ridiculous to be so easily swayed from one's indignation by a sweet word. Truly, it was.

While she grinned and said not a word, he led her into the sitting room. Not only was Mr. Bingley present as Darcy had promised, but so were Richard and Georgiana, who was accompanied by her companion, Mrs. Annesley.

"Do you not fear that my sisters will ruin your sister?" she said, attempting, once again, to convince him of his error in inviting her family to stay in his home.

"No." He said simply and led her to a settee. "We could stand at the window if you prefer," he whispered.

She shook her head and took a seat. Pacing in her father's room was one thing. Having her nervous state on display for all to see in the sitting room was something else entirely. She would summon her courage just as she always did when she was faced with a situation in which she suspected her mother or sisters would cause some embarrassment.

"All will be well," Darcy assured her softly, covering her hand, which lay on the settee, with his own.

His touch was reassuring, yet Elizabeth still sent a prayer heavenward that he was correct.

Chapter 4

For a quarter of an hour, Elizabeth engaged in conversation and allowed her mind to nearly forget the reason why they were all gathered. However, as soon as Mr. Abram, the butler, made an appearance at the door to the sitting room and Darcy rose, straightened his jacket, and extended his hand to her, the reality of the day came flooding back.

Elizabeth paused to draw a quick breath before placing her hand in Darcy's. Good. Her hand was not trembling. Her nerves must only be causing her insides to quiver.

"Mama can stay at Gracechurch Street," she whispered.

Darcy chuckled and shook his head as he wrapped her arm around his and placed her hand on his forearm. "I assure you I am made of sterner stuff than you think."

Her response of "it is not that" fell on purposefully deaf ears, and it was probably just as well. She was in danger of becoming just as annoying as her mother was when anxious, and it would not do to have Mr. Darcy think that she and her mother were alike. They were not. However, her mother had an altering effect on most people after a period of acquaintance, and as Elizabeth stood next to Darcy while the doors were opened, she hoped that whatever change her mother might work on Darcy, it would not be the sort that would drive a wedge between them. She had just begun to learn what a wonderful gentleman Darcy was, and she suspected her heart would shatter into a million pieces if he should decide that he no longer wanted her.

"Oh, Mr. Darcy," Mrs. Bennet said as she entered the house, "I must say I was delighted by your invitation to your home. Not by the circumstances that caused it, of course," she added quickly. "But the honour of being invited to stay in such a grand home as I knew yours must be — which I am now only ashamed I had not imagined to be so truly grand as it is — made the news of my husband's injury nearly bearable. I cannot tell you how often I said just such a thing to one neighbour or another as I was making preparations. It is such a noble gesture, I said. He is the most gracious gentleman, to be sure, I said. And they all agreed."

She had by this time, removed her hat and coat and was smoothing her skirts as she spoke. Then, apparently ready, she extended her hand and froze, mouth hanging slightly agape as she finally noticed her second daughter standing beside her host. She blinked as Darcy took her hand and bowed over it, extending his welcome.

"Did you have a good trip?" he asked.

Her brows furrowed, and her eyes shifted from him to Elizabeth and back. "It was excellent. There was not a thing to put us out of humour." Again, her eyes shifted to Elizabeth.

"We are glad you have joined us," Elizabeth said. "I am certain Papa will be pleased to see you."

Mrs. Bennet's brow rose. "We?"

It was one word. One short word spoken in such a tone of disbelief that Elizabeth knew her mother was beginning to put things together. And Elizabeth had to admit that it was rather tantalizingly enjoyable to be causing her mother's intrigue.

"Yes, Mr. Darcy and I as well as Aunt Addie and

Jane." She motioned toward where her sister was standing with her aunt and Bingley.

Again, Mrs. Bennet's mouth dropped open slightly before curling into a delighted smile.

"Mr. Bingley," she said, moving toward him with her hand outstretched, "it is a pleasure to see you. You have been sorely missed in Hertfordshire. But," she looked hopefully at Jane, "then it seems it was far better for you to have remained in town?"

"Oh, most certainly," Bingley replied. "I found town had just the right sort of diversion to keep me from wishing to return to Netherfield."

Mrs. Bennet clasped her hands in front of her chest. "And is there any happy news?" she asked. "My husband hinted before he left that there might be."

"Indeed, there is," Darcy replied. "However, your husband has made us promise that he be the one to share such news with you."

"He did?" Elizabeth could not catch the words before they flew from her mouth.

"Yes, my dear, he did."

Such a reply could not go unnoticed by Mrs. Bennet.

"My dear?" she cried.

Elizabeth thought from the wideness of her mother's eyes and the gasp that followed her cry of surprise, her mother might expire right there on the spot. However, she did not, and it took only a moment for the questioned words to draw a conclusion from the woman's mind.

"Oh, do not tell me," she exclaimed with obvious delight, "that Elizabeth has captured the affections of a wealthy gentleman." Her right hand tapped her chest above her heart.

"That is precisely what I have promised I would not tell you," Darcy replied. "Now, shall we move to the sitting room."

"I must see my husband," Mrs. Bennet replied. "It seems there is much he needs to tell me." Though she wore a broad smile, she was looking at Elizabeth very carefully, almost suspiciously.

"There are others for you to meet, Mama," Elizabeth said. "And Papa is sleeping."

"But my heart," she protested, tapping her chest once again.

"Your heart will survive a wait of a few moments," Mary muttered.

Mrs. Bennet glared at her third eldest daughter

but did not say a word beyond encouraging Mary, Kitty, and Lydia to follow her.

"It is good to see you, Fanny," Mrs. Gardiner said, taking her sister-in-law by the arm as they followed Darcy and Elizabeth into the sitting room. "All is very well. You shall be doubly delighted." Elizabeth heard her say.

It was just like her aunt to add a calming word when needed.

"Indeed?" her mother inquired. "Both Jane and Elizabeth?"

"Oh, that I am not supposed to say. However..."

Elizabeth looked over her shoulder just in time to see her aunt give one small sharp nod of her head which caused her mother to nearly faint away.

"Mrs. Bennet," Darcy began as soon as she and her three youngest daughters were in the sitting room, "This my cousin, the Right Honorable Colonel Richard Fitzwilliam. Richard, Mrs. Bennet, and her daughters, Miss Mary, Miss Kitty, and Miss Lydia."

Elizabeth sighed inwardly as her youngest sisters giggled softly at being presented to not just a handsome gentleman but a colonel.

"And this," Darcy continued, "is my sister, Miss

Georgiana Darcy, and her companion, Mrs. Annesley."

Mrs. Bennet did all that was proper in greeting each person, though she did keep peering curiously at Darcy and Elizabeth almost as if she needed to reassure herself that she had indeed seen what she had seen.

"Now that we have made all the proper introductions," Darcy said as Mrs. Bennet once again looked his direction, "it might be best if we see you settled into your room and allow you to check on your husband before we have tea."

"Oh, yes, indeed, Mr. Darcy, that might be the best course of action," Mrs. Bennet agreed quickly. "Not that I do not wish to make myself acquainted with your sister and the colonel," she added. "But it has been a long trip."

Elizabeth watched Darcy's lips twitch with amusement. The cunning gentleman was leading her mother down a merry path and enjoying himself thoroughly. Perhaps all would be well.

"I find I always wish for a basin of water and a fresh set of clothes after just about every journey," he said as he led her from the room and to the stairs. "While you are getting settled, I shall look in on your husband and let him know of your safe arrival."

"Yes, yes," Mrs. Bennet muttered as she looked high and low at the opulence which surrounded her. "That is a very good idea."

"And a maid can show you to his room as soon as you are ready," Darcy continued as they climbed the stairs. It was a suggestion that was met with great enthusiasm.

"Your home is so beautiful," she said as she reached the top of the stairs.

"Thank you. I hope you will also find it welcoming and comfortable."

"I cannot see how we could find it any other thing," Mrs. Bennet assured him.

"These are your rooms," Elizabeth said when they came to a stop. "This one," she said as she opened the door, "and the one next to it adjoin, and Jane and I are just across the hall."

"How lovely!" Lydia cried, pulling Kitty into the room with her.

"Your maid will conduct you to your husband as soon as you are ready, and we shall be below, awaiting your return," Darcy said. Then, with a small nod of his head in acceptance of Mrs. Bennet's words of thanks, he and Elizabeth took their leave.

"Mr. Darcy," Elizabeth said as they approached her father's room, "I must congratulate you on your cleverness. My mother's initial raptures shall be confined to this room while you avoid them in the sitting room."

He shook his head. "I fear I am not that clever, my love."

She felt her cheeks grow warm first at the appellation and then the kiss he placed on her knuckles.

"It was your father's idea. Now, shall we warn him of your mother's impending delight?" He opened the door in front of them and motioned for her to enter the room before him.

Chapter 5

"One betrothed and another nearly so," Mrs. Bennet said for the fourth time since tea had begun. She had taken a few moments to express her delight when she had arrived in the sitting room for tea. However, it had been a contained excitement for a lady so prone to exuberance as Mr. Darcy considered Mrs. Bennet to be, and then she had ventured into other topics of conversation, deftly guided by Mrs. Gardiner.

That woman still impressed Darcy each and every time he met her.

Darcy glanced at Elizabeth just as he had the three other times her mother had said such a thing. Embarrassment stained Elizabeth's cheeks and caused her head to dip, but her lips were a smile. He was almost certain he could ask for her hand now and be accepted, but he would not. Not just yet. The way she pulled her bottom lip between her teeth spoke of some worry that she still held, which he supposed was likely about how he would be able to handle her mother and sisters in large doses.

To own the truth, though he had declared he was capable of surviving the visit of the Bennets, he still held a small amount of doubt about his abilities to remain unruffled by the experience. However, when he considered that it was Elizabeth for whom he was making this effort, his confidence rose.

He smiled as she looked his direction, and she returned the gesture. Her smile was one of her most beautiful features, which was placing it at the top of a great mountain of qualities and characteristics she possessed. It lit her face and sparkled in her eyes. It even caused one brow to rise just a fraction of an inch.

He would do nearly anything for her, for he had tasted a small amount of the desolation that his life would become without her. He had not forgotten the ache that had settled into every fiber of his being as he had attempted, and failed, to forget her after leaving Netherfield. He could not, would not face such wretchedness again. He would do everything in his power to avoid it.

"Are you married?"

Lydia's question to Richard snapped Darcy from his observation of Elizabeth. What conversation had she started that he had missed while contemplating her sister?

"No," Richard replied, sparing her only a quick glance.

It was an action Darcy recognized as Richard's way to nearly ignore a female. He had seen Richard use that very technique – a half-turn of his head and a look that was not quite focused on the person who had spoken to him – when actively attempting to dissuade a young debutante from pursuing him.

"Are you courting anyone?"

Richard shook his head.

Darcy smiled. He had moved from a short reply to silence.

"Lydia." Jane hissed.

Lydia flicked her head and turned back to her tea. "Do you have a beau?" she asked Georgiana.

"Lydia," said Mrs. Gardiner, who was sitting

near her, "that is not the sort of thing one asks on first acquaintance."

"I do not," Georgiana replied with a smile for Mrs. Gardiner. "I have not had my come out just yet."

Darcy watched as Lydia's brows furrowed and her mouth dropped open.

"My sister will be presented next season. She will be well-prepared by then to present herself to the best advantage."

Lydia's head turned toward him, but she still wore her look of shocked confusion.

"There are many skills in which a young lady must be proficient before she enters the society of the ton. The expectations are great, and if not properly prepared, a young lady might have an unsuccessful first season which, in turn, might lead to her being overlooked."

"Or shunned," Georgiana replied as she nodded her head. "Last week, a particular young lady, whom I shan't name, made a grave error in refusing one gentleman at a ball and then accepting another. She has been the talk in many drawing rooms, and I fear, the subject of many jokes."

Darcy raised a brow in question. He was not certain he cared for the idea of his sister knowing such information. It smacked too much of gossip.

"Miss Allard's mother was reminding us of the rules for balls, both private and public, after we had finished our time with Mr. Hughes." She explained to her brother before she turned to Lydia. "Mr. Hughes is our dancing master." She turned back to her brother. "I would not share such a thing except it illustrated your point of being properly prepared for the season. I should not wish to make such a mistake and be the source of drawing-room tales. There are rules for a reason." Her cheeks flushed, and her head dipped but only just.

He knew she was thinking of how she had narrowly escaped being the source of many drawing-room tales. When she had been taken from school just before the events of last summer had unfolded, she had been adamant that she felt prepared for life in society. She was old enough to make her own choices. She had excelled at every lesson set before her, and she was not a foolish school girl. These things had been said with a sense of confidence. Not a word had been antagonistic. She had merely reported the facts to her brother and cousin with the hope that she would be permitted to make her debut this season. She had not been pleased to be denied the honor, but she had not pouted overly much about it — no more than Darcy expected a displeased young lady might. In fact, he had told himself that his sister had done less pouting over the disappointment than many others, such as Caroline Bingley, would have.

"I would caution you about sharing such a tale even in support of my cause," he said to her with a small smile. "However, you are correct. There are rules for a reason." He tipped his head. "When do you see Mr. Hughes next?"

"He is here tomorrow."

"And will Miss Allard be attending as well?"

Georgiana nodded.

He pursed his lips. "I wonder if it might be too much for the man to have a few more ladies to make up his sets? I know that Miss Lydia and Miss Kitty both enjoy dancing."

Lydia's eyes grew large as a smile of pure delight spread across her face. "Oh, I do. It is perhaps the very best activity in all the world, and I am quite good at it."

"What do you say, Georgiana? Do you think you

and Miss Allard would mind sharing your time with the Miss Bennets?"

Georgiana pondered the thought for only a moment before assuring one and all that a larger group would make for a much merrier lesson.

"Then, I shall send a note to Mr. Hughes today so that he might be prepared." Darcy leaned back and cradled his teacup. One activity was arranged. He would mention the theatre and the opera over dinner, and they could decide on a night for each.

He looked at Elizabeth, who was smiling at him. Yes, yes, he could do this. He just needed to keep her sisters entertained.

Chapter 6

Later that evening, Richard lowered himself into a chair near the fire in Darcy's study. Bingley sat opposite him, while Darcy pushed around a few papers on his desk, tidying up and sorting in preparation for tomorrow.

"A dance lesson is a good place to begin," Richard said after a few moments of silent relaxing before the fire. "The youngest Bennet wants some direction."

Bingley chuckled but said nothing.

Richard tapped Bingley's foot with his own. "I do not see how you can find that humorous."

Bingley lifted one shoulder and allowed it to drop but did not reply, earning him a glare.

"You are merely stating what we already know," Darcy muttered from his desk.

"You are in a position to improve them," said Richard. "Do they sing or draw?"

"I honestly do not know," Darcy answered, rising from his desk since things were in order. "It was not on my agenda to discover the skills of all the ladies in Hertfordshire when I was at Netherfield. I was there for Bingley."

"Although he did think it his duty to observe at least one lady while he was helping me."

"One is not all," Darcy replied easily as he took his seat. "They will be down in about an hour, I suspect. Mr. Bennet will be sleeping again by then." He pulled his watch from his pocket and marked the time.

"Are you not concerned about what the other Bennet ladies are about?" Richard asked.

Darcy shook his head. "No, I heard them mention some fashion magazine, and Georgiana was going to introduce them to Dash. It is not as if they are infants who need a constant nurse around them."

Richard sighed.

"Why are you so taken with them?" Bingley asked. "It is not like you to be suggesting that we try to improve young ladies. You are usually the one directing us away from the silly debutantes and hiding yourself away so that your mother will not marry you off to one of them."

"The Bennets are different." Richard shifted and stretched before looking at Darcy. "An hour, you say?"

Darcy nodded. "I should suspect they will return no sooner."

"And what will we do when they do return?"

"You are staying?" Darcy asked in surprise.

Richard nodded. "Did you not see my man? I am staying for a few days."

Richard often arrived to take up residence unannounced. So that part of his news did not surprise Darcy. However, the fact that he chose now, when the house had so many visitors, was a bit unusual.

"I thought you could use help," he said in response to Darcy's unasked question.

Darcy smiled. Richard had an uncanny way of reading people, and Darcy in particular.

"I know you do not fear for Georgiana, but I needed to see these young ladies before I could agree," Richard added. "Elizabeth was so concerned that I could not pass it off as completely ungrounded. She seems intelligent and not given to flights of fancy, and that coupled with what Jane told us about her sisters when I first met her, compelled me to decide for myself."

If it were anyone else doubting him, Darcy would have been mildly to severely irritated, but it was Richard. He might be a gentleman with a ready quip and a tease to match his nonchalant façade, but he was not the sort of gentleman to leave things to chance when there might be a better option.

"And what are your thoughts so far?" Darcy asked.

Richard grimaced and shook his head. "She inquired if I was married and if Georgie had a beau."

"Miss Lydia, you mean?" Bingley asked.

"Yes, the other two seemed less forward. Miss Mary is a trifle severe, and Miss Kitty lacks identity."

"I beg your pardon?" Bingley sat forward. "How does a lady lack identity?"

"She makes no decisions on her own," Richard replied. "She follows her younger sister. Therefore, it is the youngest that requires our attention. She is the key to the lot of them doing well or causing some calamity."

"How so?" Eager curiosity suffused Bingley's features.

"Miss Mary would do better to be less severe if she ever wishes to marry." He shuddered slightly. "She is too much of a governess." He chuckled. "Or a bit like my Aunt Catherine, and the world does not need two Lady Catherines."

"Too true," Darcy agreed with a chuckle.

"If Miss Mary did not have silly sisters of whom to disapprove constantly, she might soften her manners and her features – before that scowl becomes a permanent line between her brows." He shifted. "And if Miss Kitty is to follow, it should be someone worth following. Currently, Miss Lydia is not an appropriate leader." He sighed – a great, heavy sounding exhalation. "And I cannot explain it, but I feel as if Mrs. Bennet will calm if her daughters are all well-matched or, at least, prepared in such a fashion as to be capable of making a good match." He shrugged. "I cannot put my finger on it, but that is what my gut is saying."

Darcy propped his elbows on the arms of his chair and, steepling his fingers, rested his chin on them. If there was one thing he had learned in the past year, it was not to question Richard when he said something felt out of place or needed better scrutiny. They had both ignored the gut feeling Richard had felt regarding Mrs. Younge, Georgiana's former companion who had assisted Wickham in his attempt to persuade Georgiana into an elopement.

Richard shook his head. "She is just the sort to fall for one of Wickham's schemes."

"Mrs. Bennet?" Bingley asked in surprise.

Richard's brows furrowed as he shook his head. "No, Miss Lydia. I do not think she has the sense to see through his pretty words. She will see only his charm and handsome features and will do whatever he asks to have him as her beau. She seems rather intent upon having a beau." He might have said more but at that moment the door to the study, which was not quite closed, as Darcy had left it open to hear whatever might be happening in the hall, opened.

"No, no! Come here!"

Dash followed by a flushed Lydia, who was trailed by Kitty and Georgiana entered the room. The young ladies stopped just inside the door when they saw the gentlemen sitting within. However, Dash did not. He circled the room and then hopped onto Richard's lap without so much as a look of invitation.

"Now look here, Dash," Richard scolded as the ladies at the door giggled, "I did not ask you to accost me. Get down."

Dash immediately laid down on Richard's lap.

"That is not what I mean," Richard scolded as he rubbed the dog's ear.

"Why do you insist on petting him while reprimanding?" Darcy asked.

Richard smiled sheepishly. "How do you not scratch his ear when he looks at you with those eyes."

"I will take him," said Georgiana. "Mrs. Annesley went to her room to retrieve a particular pattern for stitching, and he scooted out with her. I do apologize." She attempted to pick Dash up from her cousin's lap, but the pup growled, causing her to pull back.

"There will be none of that," Richard said firmly and placed the dog on the floor. "No, not even those eyes will save you this time, lad."

A soft clucking and whistling drew both

Richard and Dash's attention. Lydia knelt on the floor, removing a ribbon from her hair and calling softly to Dash.

"Do you want it boy?" she asked as she wiggled the ribbon in the air. She held it toward him and then snatched it back when he put his nose forward. She repeated this three times while telling him that he only needed to come to her to have the ribbon. "Please," she added at the end of her third request.

Dash trotted to her, tail wagging, and licked her cheek when he reached her.

Lydia giggled and threw her arms around the puppy. "You cheeky fellow," she scolded while she scruffed the top of his head. "There will be no stealing kisses."

Dash paid no heed and licked her cheek again as she slipped the ribbon she held around his collar and tied it on.

"There!" she declared. "I have won this game."

The entire back half of Dash wagged with pleasure as she gave him a hug and prepared to lead him from the room.

"He seems to be taken with you, Miss Lydia," Darcy said.

"Oh, I am very good with animals," she replied. "It only takes a little persuasion – a tempting treat or toy and then praises and some attention when they respond. It is not hard." She batted her lashes.

"You did make it look easy," Bingley said.

"We will be in the drawing room in about half an hour," Darcy said to Georgiana before the ladies left.

"May we play cards?" Georgiana asked.

"I do not see why not," Darcy replied. He enjoyed a game or two of cards on occasion.

"Oh!" Lydia cried with delight as she followed Georgiana and Kitty from the study, "I am also very good with cards."

"Why do I suspect she uses some of the same techniques she used with Dash to draw gentlemen along and to win at cards?" Richard asked dryly.

Bingley chuckled. "Because, as she said, she's very good at it."

Richard shook his head. "Good she might be, but she wants instruction."

"And you wish me to provide it?" Darcy asked with a laugh.

"I cannot do it all," Richard said, rising from his

chair and straightening his jacket before brushing at the dog hair on his breeches.

"Where are you going?" Bingley asked.

Richard turned from the door. "To see that the card tables are placed and to make sure my money is well-hidden." His lips tipped up in a half smile. "I am also curious to see if Dash is still following Miss Lydia around like a green schoolboy."

Darcy looked at Bingley after Richard left the room. "Do we need to worry about him?"

Bingley nodded. "I think we may."

Chapter 7

"You do not wish to dance, Mr. Darcy?" Mrs. Bennet asked the next morning as she sipped tea and ate toast in the morning room.

Darcy had just been discussing his day with Richard, and while he had mentioned the appointment for Georgiana with her dance master, he had not included himself in the party who would be joining in on the activity.

"No, I do not," he replied simply.

"But Colonel Fitzwilliam is going to dance," Mrs. Bennet encouraged. "It would be so much more fun for the young ladies if there were two gentlemen with whom to dance. They would not have to stand up with each other for every dance that way."

"My cousin is not fond of dancing," Richard replied in Darcy's stead.

"Not fond of dancing! I declare I have never heard of such a thing."

She smiled over her cup of tea, and for a moment, Darcy saw in her eyes a familiar expressive twinkle. He had thought Elizabeth had inherited that particular impertinent expression from her father. It appeared he was wrong.

"Might you be fonder of dancing if I were to send Elizabeth to join you?" she asked.

Mrs. Bennet's lashes batted very much like Miss Lydia did when she was attempting to get her way with either dogs or humans. He had seen Lydia use that expression twice with Dash and at least as many times with Richard while playing cards last evening. The shock of the similarity between Mrs. Bennet and both her second eldest and youngest daughters slowed the smile that curled his lips at such a suggestion.

"I do find it more enjoyable to dance with Miss Elizabeth than anyone else," he admitted, causing Richard to laugh, and Mrs. Bennet to beam.

"Then, I will send her to you."

"Only if she is amenable," Darcy cautioned. "I would not wish to force her to do that which she does not wish to do."

At this Mrs. Bennet giggled, and then, with a slight arch to her right eyebrow — very reminiscent, in Darcy's mind, to another expression of Elizabeth's — she responded in a whisper, "I should not say it, for I would not wish to hinder your regard for her, but there are few who can force Elizabeth to do that which she does not wish to do. She is a very determined young lady and has been so since before she was in leading strings."

To Darcy's surprise, there was a look of pride on the woman's face that seemed to run contrary to her disparaging words.

"Her father has taught her to use that determination to great effect, though I find there is still room for improvement. Elizabeth is not one to be swayed by pretty words and affected airs as some might be. And that is a very good quality for a young lady to possess." She took a sip of her tea. "One does not wish to be tricked into believing things that are not so." She sighed. "I am not so good at that sort of thing as is my husband. That is why he has worked so diligently with Elizabeth. I am certain I would have failed her, for she is far more challenging than any of my other daughters."

"Miss Lydia seems to be in need of some similar instruction," Richard muttered.

Mrs. Bennet's brows rose as did Darcy's. Richard was not usually one to be so open about his disapproval of someone.

"I fear she might fall prey to some of the charmers here in town," he added.

"Do you really think so?"

There was no denying the genuine fear which coloured Mrs. Bennet's tone.

Richard nodded. "I do."

"But she is a sly one," Mrs. Bennet said. "Lydia knows far more than she will ever display. She does not wish to be thought a bluestocking, you see."

Richard's expression did not register belief. "Be that as it may," he said, "you must admit her head is easily turned by a handsome gentleman. She has spoken of little else. Gentlemen, beaus, ribbons, and dresses – and the ribbons and dresses were only mentioned in terms of capturing a beau."

Mrs. Bennet huffed, and Darcy, picking up his cup, leaned back in his chair to watch.

"It is imperative for a young lady to be fashionably attired to show not only her status but also to entice a gentleman to make an offer." Mrs. Bennet wore a stern look as she shook her head. "Any lady's future is dependent upon securing the best offer, and a lady who has little to her name aside from the claim of a gentleman father must make the best use of what is available to her in seeking a secure future."

Richard's head cocked to the side as he studied the woman before him for a full thirty ticks of the clock on the side table. Then, he nodded. "I will agree that what you say is true if you will agree that the young lady in question needs guidance to guarantee that the gentleman who calls on her is not a cad presenting himself as a proper match."

Mrs. Bennet blinked, but then lifted her chin. "I am certain all of my daughters would be able to pick out a cad should one present himself."

Richard shook his head. "They have not. I know it for a fact."

"You cannot know that!" Indignation radiated off Mrs. Bennet in palpable waves.

"What do you think of Mr. Wickham?"

Darcy nearly choked on his tea at the question.

"He is a handsome fellow, very pleasant and promising."

Richard shrugged. "He is handsome and pleasant, but he is only promising if you wish to win his money in a game of card. However, if you are a merchant expecting repayment or a lady expecting an offer of marriage and not just a bit of fun, especially if you have no fortune, he is quite the opposite of promising."

Mrs. Bennet huffed. "He cannot be. Elizabeth found him agreeable."

"We all err at times," Richard said softly. "But, I know for a fact that he is nothing more than a practiced liar and a libertine."

"But Lizzy is always right." Mrs. Bennet's brows were drawn together so tightly that they nearly touched.

"What was her opinion of my cousin?" Richard asked.

Mrs. Bennet's brows sprang apart and upward as she turned wide eyes toward Darcy.

"I was less than civil," Darcy said. "Her opinion was not without justification."

"True," Richard agreed. "But it still stands to reason that she is just as fallible as the rest of us. A person presents himself in a particular manner, and we all determine he is a particular sort of person until evidence refutes our evaluation."

Mrs. Bennet's brows were once again furrowed, and her face was suffused with confusion.

"He means," Darcy began, drawing the woman's attention back to himself, "that until I presented myself as civil and gentlemanly, your daughter saw me as a dour disapproving man, which I was. I did not behave at all as I should have while in Hertfordshire. I have apologized to her, but I should also apologize to you for speaking of your daughter as I did at the assembly. It was wrong. She is lovely and very handsome."

Mrs. Bennet smiled. "I knew you could not be an utter fool. You would have to sooner or later admit that she was pretty, for she is. Perhaps not so handsome as Jane, but Elizabeth is far more than tolerable."

"I would agree." Though his cheeks were warm from the reprimand in her words, he could not help but smile at her assessment of Elizabeth. "She is far more than tolerable. However, getting back to my cousin's point, even if I would find it far more entertaining to contemplate your daughter..."

At that, Mrs. Bennet giggled.

"Mr. Wickham will present himself as an affable gentleman until he has acquired whatever it is that he wishes. Only then will his true character be revealed." Darcy's brows furrowed. He could not tell her about his sister's ordeal, but there must be some bit of information that would help her understand Wickham's lack of character. "What do you know about him?"

She shrugged. "He mentioned he was a friend of your family, but beyond that..." Her eyes grew wide, and she gasped. "Very little," she admitted quietly.

"He was a friend of my family. In fact, he was a favourite of my father. So much so that when my father died, Mr. Wickham was bequeathed one thousand pounds and, should he take orders, the living at Kympton, which was in my father's power to bestow when a vacancy should arise. There are many details that I could add, but I will suffice it to say that the living was refused in favour of three thousand pounds."

"He squandered it," Richard interrupted. "Four thousand pounds gone in a very short period of licentious living."

"Can this be true?"

Darcy could not fault Mrs. Bennet for being so surprised. Wickham was very good at weaving a tale and presenting himself in the best light. "I fear it is. Again, there is more I could tell you, but not without endangering the reputation of a young lady whom we – my cousin and I – know."

Her eyes grew wide. "Did..." she looked around the room and lowered her voice, "did he ruin her?"

Darcy shook his head. "Thankfully, no, but he played with her heart in hopes of securing her dowry."

Mrs. Bennet's hand flew to her mouth as her eyes filled with tears. It was a response which Darcy had not fully expected. Surprise was to be expected, but tears? He saw her jaw clench and relax before she swallowed and spoke softly but with a great deal of anger behind her words.

"From this moment, he is no longer a friend of mine. The heart is a precious thing, and its ruin is..." She shook her head and brushed a tear from her cheek. "What can be done for my Lydia? She is very taken with Mr. Wickham."

"If you allow me, I shall consider it and devise a plan," Richard said. "There must be at least one young man in London who could replace Wickham in Miss Lydia's regard. Between Darcy and I, and with Bingley's assistance, I am certain we can help her forget Wickham."

Relief washed over Mrs. Bennet's whole being. "I would be so delighted if you would."

Chapter 8

A vision in a blue day dress stood in the corridor. Darcy paused for a moment to appreciate her form as she was unaware of his presence; then he continued toward his destination.

"Miss Elizabeth."

Darcy smiled as he said her name in greeting. Seeing her here in his home was such a pleasure, but she did not have to be present for him to wear this particular smile. Just the thought of her brought a great deal of joy to him. How very different from just a few weeks ago when he thought of her only with sorrow as he contemplated a long and dreary existence without her in his life. Happily, he had been guided by his friend to rethink his position, and now, here he was standing just outside the ballroom — his ballroom — with her.

"Mr. Darcy," she said, returning his smile and

dipping a small curtsey. "My mother informs me that I am to participate in a dance lesson?"

"Only if you wish to do so."

Elizabeth laughed lightly. "My mother was most insistent that I wished to dance, and my father agreed! I should not like to return to them and tell them I have not danced."

"But you do not wish to dance?" Darcy's brows rose. He thought she loved dancing.

Her lips twitched as she attempted to affect a serious expression, but it was of no use. She could not keep her amusement from showing on her face. "I would so like to tease that I despise dancing, but I fear I am not so good an actress as that. I do love to dance."

Darcy offered his arm. "Then shall we interrupt and join the fun?"

Her left eyebrow lifted impertinently, and she opened her mouth to speak. However, Darcy spoke first.

"Your mother does that very thing," he said, looking steadfastly at her face as if he had never before seen her. And for a moment, he felt as if he had not. He was not certain how many times he had felt this very same way — as if he was seeing things for the first time — since that moment in Bingley's study when he had confessed first to his part in separating his friend from Jane and then to loving Elizabeth. He needed to pay better attention to people. He had always thought himself a good observer and reader of character, but at present, he found himself wanting.

Elizabeth's brows furrowed. "What does my mother do?"

He had turned to look at her more fully, lifting her hand from his arm and placing it in his left hand before he ran a finger of his right hand over her left brow. "She lifts this very same brow just as you were doing a moment ago. I assume you were about to tease me." He smiled at her, his hand resting on her cheek. "You often arch that brow when you are about to say something impertinent. It is an enchanting expression. One of many."

She was so beautiful. Her eyes, her lips, and even her nose spoke as plainly as her words did.

"You fascinate me," he muttered.

Her lips were parted as if she wanted to speak but no words would form.

He caressed that one eyebrow once more and

then removed his hand from her face. "What were you about to say?"

She shook her head. "I do not know."

"Then shall we join the others and dance?"

Her eyes grew wide.

"You remember," he said with a smile.

"I do." Her lips curled into a smile, and that one eyebrow arched as he waited and watched.

"I was going to say I had thought you did not like to dance, Mr. Darcy."

He could not help himself. He had to touch her cheek again as he responded, "I like to dance with you."

Her cheeks flushed, and her lids lowered as she looked away from his eyes. "There will be others with whom to dance. You shall not be allowed to dance only with me."

He waited until her eyes lifted to his again before speaking. "The prize is worth the price." It was enjoyable making her lower her eyes and smile that soft smile she was wearing now. "Come, my love. Let us disturb the master."

Inside the ballroom, Lydia, Miss Allard, Richard, Georgiana, Kitty, and Mary were just forming sets.

"Ah! Do we have more dancers?" The slight,

blonde-haired master cried in delight, clapping his hands together.

"Miss Elizabeth, this is Mr. Hughes. Mr. Hughes, Miss Elizabeth Bennet."

The man bowed and welcomed Elizabeth.

"Do you dance well?" he asked.

"She dances very well," Darcy said. "I have had few partners who performed better."

Mr. Hughes clapped his hands in delight once more, chortling about his good fortune to have such assistance in instructing his pupils. "An example to follow is far superior to attempting to follow my words. You will stand up together, yes?" he asked, looking from Darcy to Elizabeth and back.

"With pleasure," Darcy assured him. He had always found Mr. Hughes to be a most animated fellow, but today with a room full of dancers, the man was positively beside himself with glee that showed in his every movement and expression.

Mr. Hughes tapped his lip with his finger as he surveyed the room. Then, he flitted over to the group of dancers.

"Here. You will do well to be near Miss Allard

and Miss Kitty. Miss Darcy and Miss Mary will stand beside Colonel Fitzwilliam and Miss Lydia."

After Darcy and Elizabeth had taken their places, he clapped his hands three times, pulled himself straighter, and said, "Ladies, I expect great things from you today with so many fine examples to follow." Then, he nodded to his assistant, who began to play the cotillion, *Le Rouët à filer*.

"Circle right," he called as he clapped his hands in time to the music. "No, no, no! Join hands behind. Behind, Miss Mary. Not in front. Ah, better."

And so it continued for a full three repetitions of the same cotillion before the second and final dance of the day, a quadrille was attacked in the same fashion with instructions such as forward, back, and step lightly being given over the music.

Finally, as the second attempt of the quadrille came to an end, Mr. Hughes clapped loudly and shouted, "Well done! Well done! A fabulous day. Simply fabulous."

Darcy chuckled. The gentleman's fair complexion was nearly as flushed as Miss Lydia's who wore a smile as broad as Mr. Hughes did. There was no denying that Miss Lydia found dancing to be the best activity in the world when her enjoyment was so evidently displayed.

"Can we not dance one more?" Lydia asked.

"I am afraid I must be on to another appointment," Mr. Hughes replied. "However, if it is possible, I would welcome you to join me again for a lesson. You are very light and quick on your feet, and so graceful."

Lydia sighed and thanked him, though it was apparent to anyone who looked at her that she was disappointed that Mr. Hughes was leaving.

"Come, Miss Lydia, allow the gentleman to leave," instructed Richard.

Lydia sighed again, a small pout forming on her lips. "If I must."

"You must."

Richard's assurance was met with another sigh.

He pulled his watch from his pocket. "What would you say to taking Dash for a walk?"

Lydia's eyes lit with delight. "I should like that very much."

"Darcy?" Richard asked.

"I see no folly in such a plan as long as Dash's leash is secure." The animal would likely benefit from expending some of his energy in a walk.

"And will you join us?" Richard asked.

Darcy looked at Elizabeth and after getting a nod in response to his unasked question, told Richard that in half an hour's time, they would all take Dash for a walk.

Chapter 9

Dash paced the drawing room, stopping to sniff each person, and thoroughly checking each corner before he decided to curl up at Lydia's feet.

Darcy shook his head, both Dash and his cousin had been following Lydia around all day. First, it was the dance lesson – Dash was, thankfully, absent for that. Then, it was their walk where Lydia had one hand on Dash's leash and the other on Richard's arm. After that, they had spent a bit of time in the music room with Georgiana, where it was discovered that Lydia had a most remarkable voice, though she could not play a single song without several stumbles. For dinner, Dash had once again been relegated to his room, but now, as they sat in the drawing room, he was at his favourite Miss Bennet's feet, and Richard was at her side.

"She seems very willing to listen to everything the Colonel says," Jane whispered to Elizabeth with a nod toward Lydia.

"Indeed, she does. It is most remarkable," Elizabeth replied. "He suggests, and she does. I have never seen her so compliant." She darted her eyes toward Darcy before continuing. "Do you suspect she has set her cap at him? He is unattached."

Jane sighed. "I would say yes if she were to act more..."

A loud giggle cut off Jane's words.

Jane's shoulders drooped, and she changed her answer to a simple yes as she saw her youngest sister playfully swat Richard's arm.

Oh, that was not good. Elizabeth watched Lydia duck her head and bat her eyes. Surely, the colonel would not be swayed by such obvious ploys. He had navigated the ton for many years and yet remained unmarried. He was far too sensible and astute a gentleman to be led along by a pretty young girl, especially one so young as Lydia, was he not?

"I think she fascinates him," Darcy whispered. "He wishes to see her improved," he added when both Jane and Elizabeth turned shocked eyes toward him.

Elizabeth bit her lip. "It is a dangerous game they play."

"How so?" Darcy asked.

"Affections could be aroused without a hope of a future." She spoke softly as she did not wish to have anyone other than Darcy and Jane hear what she had to say.

"You fear Richard will engage your sister's heart with no intention of returning her admiration?"

That was part of it, though she did not expect the colonel to do so knowingly.

"He might also find himself enamoured. It is less likely, but not outside the realm of possibility."

"And if both should become attached, what harm would there be?"

Darcy's brows were furrowed, and to Elizabeth, he looked less than pleased.

"I do not mean to imply that I would object to such a thing, but how could it be resolved happily? I do not know your cousin's situation, but my sister has little..." she grimaced at the next word, "money." It sounded so callous, so avaricious. It felt no better to add her next thoughts. "His father is an earl. Our father is little-known."

"My uncle is an earl," Darcy replied. "Yet, I would happily marry one of your father's daughters."

Elizabeth's brows furrowed. "But it is different," she protested, though she was uncertain how to put it into words. "He is a son. Would his father even approve?"

Darcy shrugged. "Richard is not known for doing things just to please anyone. He is his own man."

"But his inheritance could be threatened."

How could he not see that the colonel pursuing a young lady such as Lydia would be disadvantageous and... well... wrong? That thought brought to mind something about which Elizabeth had been wondering since the day her father had fallen while they toured Darcy's grand home.

"I still do not know why you would choose someone like me when you have so much, and I have so little."

"You are not a pauper begging for food on the street," he replied with a smile. "Your family is not poor."

Her cheeks grew warm. "No, we are not, but compared to this," she indicated the room by looking around, "we are not equals."

"Very well, if you are using things such as money as the measurement for equality of station, then no, we are not equals. However, you are a gentleman's daughter. I am a gentleman's son."

"Yes, but.."

"And I love you," he said, cutting off her words. "As you already know, that is the determining factor as to why I choose you. You may thank Bingley for making me aware of such reasoning, and you may also take up your argument with him if you find the reasoning unfounded."

Were he not smiling while lifting those brows so imperiously, and had he not just declared he loved her – and before her sister — Elizabeth might have been put out with his final words. As it was, all she could do was smile that silly grin, just as she always did when he said something sweet, and think of no logical retort. How did one refute a declaration of love?

"I will admit that my cousin has always said he would marry to better his lot in life," Darcy said when Elizabeth remained silent. "And it would weigh on him to have his inheritance threatened, I will not deny those facts. However, I would not see him do without, and I know he would not desert a lady he loved just for a few more pounds from some other source. He is too honorable for that."

"Which proves my point exactly," Elizabeth declared. "It is a dangerous game they play. How could such a future be happy?"

"You ask the wrong question."

The wrong question? Surely, not. If the colonel and Lydia were to fall in love and wish to marry, there would be strictures placed on them by lack of wealth that would most certainly lead to eventual discontent and therefore, unhappiness.

"I cannot see how I have asked amiss," Elizabeth replied. "Strictures and a reduction in means of living would not sit well with either your cousin or my sister."

Darcy shook his head and smiled.

Was he dismissing her opinion as foolish? She knew her point was valid.

"The question one should ask," he began, still wearing that amused smile, "is not how could their future be happy together in the reduced circumstances you fear, but rather, how could their future be happy without the one whom they love. I pondered that very thing for weeks before Bingley so wisely pointed out the error in my thinking."

Elizabeth knew she was smiling that silly smile again. It was ridiculous how easily her emotions could be swayed whenever he even hinted at loving her.

"But you are wealthy," she protested. Charming words and whether she felt compelled to smile instead of scowl, did not change the fact that she knew she was correct.

"My cousin is not poor. He is just not as wealthy as he would wish to be."

She lifted her chin. "I still say it is a dangerous game."

"Say what you will, but I will say that it is not so dangerous as you think. And on this, I shall not be moved."

She shook her head and turned away from Darcy's charming smile. She would press her point no further. It was so much easier to debate with him when he was being dour — not that she had any desire for him to become dour once again.

Time and experience would have to determine the winner of this contest, and as Lydia once again giggled at something the colonel said, Elizabeth hoped that she might be proven wrong. For though Lydia was a trial at times, Elizabeth did not wish to see her sister injured, and from the way, Lydia was looking at Colonel Fitzwilliam, injury was indeed a possibility, whether Mr. Darcy chose to acknowledge it or not.

Chapter 10

The next morning, as Darcy once again started the summation of a column through which he had only made it halfway before finding his mind wandering back to Elizabeth and their conversation about Lydia and Richard, the door opened, and he acknowledged the entrance of his cousin with a nod of his head.

"Miss Lydia seems enamoured with you," he said, glancing up from his books as his cousin settled into a chair. That column of numbers seemed destined to remain as they were – without a total at the bottom. "You are only encouraging proper behaviour and not encouraging an attachment, are you not?"

One corner of his cousin's mouth tipped up, causing Darcy to pause and lay his pen aside. Yes, those numbers would remain without a total for a while longer.

"She is a pretty thing," Richard finally replied.

"And young. And not an heiress."

Richard shrugged and sighed. "True."

"But?" Darcy prodded. Richard rarely capitulated so easily.

Richard shook his head. "I do not know."

Darcy knew just how quickly a gentleman could fall for a pretty Bennet lady. Bingley had been lost before the end of one dance, and he, himself, had not been a whole lot longer in falling for Elizabeth. He had just fought the reality of such a thing happening where his friend had readily accepted it.

The fact that his cousin, who was never without a plan of which he knew the workings forward and back, was currently faltering when answering a question about his plan to improve Lydia Bennet spoke loudly to Darcy that Richard's heart might likely be in danger of being lost.

"She is Georgiana's age," Darcy continued.

Richard nodded. "And in one year's time, Georgiana will be entertaining gentlemen in the sitting room and dancing with them at balls."

"But she will be a year older," Darcy argued. He

leaned back in his chair and studied his cousin. It was not that Darcy did not wish for Richard to find a lady who made him happy, nor was his argument actually about Lydia's age. I was more about the fact that he had always thought a more mature and sensible sort of lady would catch Richard's eye. In fact, he had not truly believed that his cousin was in danger last evening when speaking with Elizabeth. A small niggling worry had poked him a time or two, but he had brushed it away each time it did. However, this morning while having his first cup of tea, he had reconsidered his talk with Elizabeth and had decided the best thing to do was to broach the subject with his cousin rather than just guess and suppose.

Richard threw one leg over the other. "Do not fear. I have not lost my heart to Miss Lydia's pretty blue eyes. I am merely helping her achieve her potential, so that she can find a proper husband. I am, after all, married to my profession."

"It concerns me that you know the colour of her eyes," Darcy muttered, causing Richard to laugh.

"I notice things about people."

"Especially if the person is a pretty young lady," Darcy added.

"They are more pleasant to observe than some dour old gent."

Darcy was about to give a final word of caution when Abrams knocked and entered.

"You have callers, sir," said the butler. "Miss Bingley and Sir Matthew are awaiting you in the sitting room. Mrs. Bennet is entertaining them until you arrive."

"And the Miss Bennets?" Darcy rose from his desk and donned his jacket.

"The youngest are with Miss Darcy and Mrs. Annesley. The eldest are with their father."

"If the eldest could be spared from their father's side, Miss Bingley might wish to see them."

He pulled at his sleeves and straightened his waistcoat as Mr. Abrams left the study. Mrs. Bennet was not unfamiliar with entertaining guests in her home. He did not need to rush to see to his callers, yet he felt as if he should. Miss Bingley was not favourably disposed to any of the Bennets – especially after the incident at the Johnson's ball. In fact, he was surprised she had called at his home at all. He had hoped she would be too put out with him and his part in the fiasco leading to her current betrothed state to call on him. His cheeks puffed out as he exhaled.

"This should be entertaining," Richard said from directly next to Darcy, causing him to jump.

"It might well be. I wonder why she has decided to call?"

"Only one way to find out." Richard held the door for his cousin to exit before him.

In the sitting room, Caroline Bingley was perched on the edge of a settee with Sir Matthew at her side. She wore a green gown and a tight smile. There was nothing relaxed in her form at all. She was not, Darcy decided, here of her own accord. He would like to know just how Sir Matthew, who was, as always, relaxed and unruffled, managed to get her to Darcy House.

"Hurst told me that your husband had been injured," Caroline was saying to Mrs. Bennet as Darcy entered. "And Sir Matthew and I, of course, thought it only proper to call to inquire after his health." She paused and raised her chin slightly. "We are to be relations, after all."

"You are too good, Miss Bingley. I had not thought to see you at all while I was in town. I said to Lady Lucas that it would be delightful to see you, but I did not expect it. You would be busy with the season and all that I told her. Yet, here you are. Quite a proper thing, and so kind. Mr. Bennet is resting well, and we hope he will be able to return to Longbourn in just over a week. There have been no complications, no fever, no swoons, or anything else. We have been quite blessed."

Darcy slipped into a chair while Mrs. Bennet spoke.

"Oh, Mr. Darcy," Mrs. Bennet cried upon noticing him, "Is it not just the best treat ever to have Miss Bingley call on us?"

Darcy bit back a smile at how the lady had joined herself to his establishment and referred to him and her as "us." "Indeed, it is."

"And she has the most wonderful news."

"Does she?"

"She does!"

Mrs. Bennet's face was suffused with excitement.

"She is betrothed!"

Again, Darcy bit back a smile as he replied, "I had heard that she was." He darted a look toward Caroline, who, catching his eye, glared at him.

"And to a baronet! Oh, she is a most fortunate

lady." Mrs. Bennet gasped. "Lady Broadhurst! How well that sounds! You must be delighted," she said to Caroline before gasping once again. "Forgive me, I have quite forgotten my manners in light of such wonderful news. Do you know Sir Matthew, Mr. Darcy?"

Darcy nodded. "I do."

Mrs. Bennet looked relieved. "Lady Broadhurst," she muttered once again. "I should be very pleased if any of my daughters were ever to have such a title. Miss Bingley, you have done very well, very well, indeed."

To Darcy's surprise, Caroline's smile shifted from the tight one she had been wearing to one of a lady who was quite pleased with herself.

"I have done well, have I not?" she agreed.

The look she gave Darcy was nearly his undoing, but he bit his cheek and kept his composure. Apparently, Mrs. Bennet's praise of Caroline's status had been a balm capable of changing the glare Caroline had given him before into a look of mild hauteur. While he did not appreciate how she looked down her nose at him, he was relieved to see her more relaxed posture.

"I do believe it is I who has done very well." Sir

Matthew sat forward and covered Caroline's hand with one of his.

To Darcy's surprise, Caroline Bingley blushed and dipped her head. If he had not seen it with his own eyes, he would not have believed it possible should someone tell him of it. Sir Matthew had said he thought his odds were good in persuading Caroline to love him, and it appeared he was right.

Richard leaned toward Darcy. "Remind me never to play cards with that man."

Darcy chuckled. "I asked that Miss Bennet and Miss Elizabeth be made aware of your arrival."

Caroline's eyes grew wide. "You did?"

"Yes, I thought you might like to visit with them."

"Of course, we would," answered Sir Matthew. "I should like to get to know them better, especially Miss Bennet as she will be a sister."

"Is that not wonderful?" cried Mrs. Bennet. "I thought for sure when Mr. Bingley left Netherfield, and then his sisters and Mr. Darcy followed, that my Jane would be forgotten." Her brows and chin rose. "Not that any of my daughters are easily forgotten." She shook her head. "But I did think we had lost Mr. Bingley, and he had shown such promise. He is such an amiable gentleman," she directed this last bit to Sir Matthew, "just the sort of gentleman with whom a mother wishes for her daughter to be happily settled."

"And his fortune is not small." Caroline's lashes fluttered as she smiled at Mrs. Bennet.

"Oh, it is not, you are most correct, but then you should be as you are his sister and more intimately acquainted with such things," Mrs. Bennet replied. "A mother does like to see her daughters well-situated. You will understand when you have a daughter or two of your own. It is such a worry. Why a lady's future rest entirely on that very thing – finding, as you have done, a gentleman to lend his rank and keep her in dresses and a home."

Clearly, from the shocked look on Caroline's face, Mrs. Bennet's answer had not been what she had expected. To own the truth, it was not what Darcy had expected either, but it did, strangely, make him happy to be one of the gentlemen who would care for the future of one of Mrs. Bennet's daughters.

Chapter 11

"I hear Miss Bingley called." Mr. Bennet pushed himself up, pulling his leg along the bed while taking great pains not to move it any more than was necessary to achieve a comfortable sitting position.

"She did," Darcy replied. "Sir Matthew seems quite capable of steering her in the proper direction." Seeing the curiosity on Mr. Bennet's face, he added, "He covers her hand, drawing her attention away from whatever she is about to set upon as a topic of conversation; he replies before she does when there is a danger that her answer might not be pleasing; and he stays as close to her side as is possible. It is remarkable actually. If you were not looking for such actions, one would never suspect he is directing her."

"And does she seem to be warming to him?" Mr. Bennet winced as he shifted once again. "I promise it does not hurt as it did, but there are moments when that injury reminds me it is there."

Darcy smiled apologetically. "Is there anything I can get you for your comfort?"

Mr. Bennet began to shake his head but then stopped as a small smile crept onto his lips. "You could marry my daughter. I should be very comfortable knowing my Lizzy was well-settled."

"I should like to oblige you as soon as possible. However, your daughter is not yet ready for such a discussion. And, to be fair, we are only just becoming well-acquainted." Darcy's comments were met with a resigned sigh.

"I would say that you have all your life to become acquainted after you marry, but..." he paused and looked toward the far corner of the room where a dressing table stood next to a large wardrobe, "sometimes even twenty-three years is not enough for some to learn what they should know about their mate." He drew a deep breath and expelled it. "Though I love her, my wife may never understand me." He shook his head. "Courting for a year rather than just a week and three days would not have changed that fact."

He turned back to Darcy. "It would have, however, helped me prepare for what lay ahead. I knew my Fanny did not possess a keen wit, but I had not accepted that it was part and parcel of who she was. I thought it could be changed." Again, he shook his head. "It seems it cannot be."

He looked down at the blue blanket which lay across his lap and ran his hands over it as if smoothing some imaginary wrinkles from it. "I should have been like Sir Matthew. He knows his future wife's failings, and as you said, he is taking steps to direct them."

Darcy did not know how to respond to such an admission, but he did not have to, as Mr. Bennet continued.

"When we first married, I attempted to engage Fanny's mind. I read her books and asked her questions, but my efforts fell on deaf ears or a dull mind. I tried teasing and prodding. However, she did not know that she needed to move, and so she did not. That is when I retreated to find solace in my solitude and to hide my failure in laughter." He shook his head. "Do not do that. Remember our discussion at the ball – when I said a gentleman who is rarely rattled by anything might become indifferent to those things which should stir him to action?"

Darcy nodded.

"My strength of forbearance became indolence." Mr. Bennet chuckled. "One has a great deal of time to ponder things, when he is confined to his bed, and a tendency to become contemplative, when his daughters are on the verge of beginning their own families. But enough of that. Did you not say you had a chessboard somewhere?"

"I did."

"Then, might not you go retrieve it so we can have something to do while listening to me meander down my ruminative road?"

Darcy chuckled and rose to call for the chess set.

"How are my daughters?" Mr. Bennet asked when Darcy returned to his chair. "Not my eldest, but my youngest."

"They seem to be settling into their new surroundings well." He paused and grimaced slightly. "I fear I am not the best at entertaining young ladies. We have had a dance lesson and a walk. Tomorrow, I believe, there is talk of a shopping excursion."

This news did not seem to be news at all to Mr.

Bennet as he simply nodded and said, "Will you accompany them?"

Darcy shook his head. "Mrs. Annesley will be with my sister, so there is no need for me to attend them. As I heard it, they are only looking for gloves and a pair of slippers for Georgiana."

This was met with a burst of laughter. "I should be surprised if that is the extent of their purchases. My wife is not known for her restraint, and shopping is one of the skills at which she excels."

"My aunt is the same," Darcy replied. "My uncle is forever bemoaning the bills for dresses and hats and the need to redo this or that room. My aunt will hear some bit of news about the latest thing and find it necessary to be the first to adopt it."

"That is not unlike my wife."

The chess set arrived just then, and they paused their conversation while it was set up on a table next to the bed.

"I fear I will not be able to reach every spot," Mr. Bennet said as he surveyed the board.

"Just instruct me on what move you wish to make, and I will see it done. You may begin."

"You never told me if Miss Bingley was warming

to Sir Matthew," Mr. Bennet said as he made his first move.

Darcy tipped his head to the left and then the right as he decided which piece to move first. "She blushed and dipped her head more than once at something the man said or did. I do believe he is in a good way of finding himself well liked if not loved."

"Ah, that is good to hear. Felicity in marriage is a wonderful thing."

"I believe you have the right of it," Darcy agreed.

For five minutes the only sound that could be heard in the room was the moving of pieces and the occasional direction of Mr. Bennet as to which piece needed to be placed where when he could not reach to do it himself.

"Returning to my daughters," Mr. Bennet said, breaking the concentration on the game before them, "my Lydia seems enamoured with your cousin, but then she is easily swayed by a uniform."

Mr. Bennet's hand rested on his knight, but he did not move it. "Lizzy says the admiration may not all be on one side." He lifted his horse and placed it ahead and to the left, blocking the advancement of Darcy on his queen.

Again, Darcy's head tipped to the side as he attempted to figure out the best way to get around Mr. Bennet's pieces. "Richard assures me he is only interested in seeing Lydia improve."

"He thinks she wants improvement?"

Darcy swallowed. Perhaps that had not been the best way to respond to the man's question. He nodded. "Yes." What else could he say and remain honest?

"He's not wrong. Did he say why he thought she needed improvement?"

Darcy blew out a breath. "She asked him nearly upon her arrival if he was married and then proceeded to inquire after any beaus my sister might have."

Mr. Bennet made a dissatisfied sound.

"He worries that she would be an easy conquest for a man such as Wickham. There are several of only marginally better morals in town."

"Is that all?"

As Darcy took his turn, he heard the disbelief in the question and felt rather than saw the scrutiny he was receiving from Mr. Bennet. He shook his head. "Richard also feels that Miss Mary would have less to criticize, and Miss Kitty would have a better example to follow if Miss Lydia were to improve. That is why he selected her as the object of his instruction."

He looked up to see Mr. Bennet still pondering him.

"It does not hurt that she has pretty blue eyes," Darcy added.

Mr. Bennet chuckled. "He noticed her eyes, did he?"

Darcy responded with a small shrug and a nod.

"What if he did find her more than just an object of curiosity and a project?" Mr. Bennet asked, leaning back on his pillows, the game forgotten for a moment.

"He is an honorable gentleman if that is what you are asking."

"In part, yes. But what of his future?"

"You mean money?"

Mr. Bennet nodded. "He is a second son, and my daughter has little in the way of wealth. Lydia is not a pauper, but she is not the sort someone in the colonel's position might seek out."

Darcy drew and expelled a deep breath. "He is not without funds and a home. He will also have his retirement once he leaves his position – if he leaves his position – in his majesty's service."

"He is happy in his profession then?"

Darcy nodded. "He seems to be, and there is talk of him joining himself to a position here in town. He has not said more than it would keep him on home soil."

"Nothing is guaranteed in this day and age with so much unrest," Mr. Bennet said solemnly.

"True."

Mr. Bennet leaned forward and moved a piece. "Check."

"Mate," said Darcy after looking at his options to try to escape capture and realizing there were none.

"Oh, well, will you look at that? You are right. I had not thought you so captured. I shall blame that oversight on the laudanum," said Mr. Bennet with a chuckle.

Chapter 12

Elizabeth wandered around the library, looking first at this book and then that one. There were definitely enough books here to keep her entertained for some months if not years. Some she had read, a few she was certain she never wished to read, and others called to her to pick them up and read them immediately. She sighed. It was as if she had been presented with a full tray of her favourite sweets. How did one select just the right delectable treat?

She moved a few feet from the shelves on the left side of the room to where a large globe stood just at the edge of a group of chairs. Her head tipped to the side, and she leaned forward as she spun the globe slowly, looking at the various forms on it. How she would like to have one of these to look at all the time. She smiled. If she married Mr. Darcy, she would, or at least, she would when they were in residence here.

"I thought I might find you here," Jane said, as she closed the door softly behind her.

"Is this not the most beautiful room?" Elizabeth extended her hands and twirled in a circle.

Jane wrinkled her nose. "You know I do not like reading so much as you do. Therefore, I cannot agree that this is the most beautiful room, for I find many other rooms to be just as inviting." She stood next to her sister, and while Elizabeth huffed her disagreement, she wrapped her arm around Elizabeth's and began leading her around the room.

"If you do not wish to read, then why are you here?"

"To disturb you," Jane replied with a laugh, "and to retrieve a book. Just because I do not enjoy reading as much as you do, does not mean I do not read." She squeezed her sister's arm and lowered her voice. "This could be your library."

"I was just pondering that very thing." Elizabeth felt her cheeks grow warm at the admission.

"So do you love him?" Jane's whispered question was full of hopeful excitement.

It was not the first time, Jane had asked that

question of Elizabeth. She had asked it many times since that night at the Johnson's ball. To own the whole truth, Jane had even asked if Elizabeth could love Mr. Darcy before the ball, but it was not until after her reintroduction to Mr. Darcy at that ball when Elizabeth felt it to be a distinct possibility.

"I like him very much," Elizabeth hedged.

"Like? Only like?" Shock and censure coloured Jane's response.

"Very much," Elizabeth repeated before adding two steps later, "and maybe more."

It was the closest she had come to acknowledging what she suspected her heart was telling her. She was uncertain why she could not just admit that she loved Mr. Darcy, but it seemed too grave a thing to declare without proper consideration.

"He loves you."

"I know."

"He has been very good with Mama and our sisters."

"They have only just arrived."

Jane stopped walking and pulled Elizabeth to a settee. "You will not be living with Mama once you are married. Even if Papa were to die, you would not have to house her very often. You will be so far away, and you know how she is about travelling more than a day's journey. She will not wish to make that trip very often, for it will require staying at an inn."

Their mother had a great dislike of staying anywhere that was not the home of a friend or a relation. She worried about being robbed or murdered as well as contracting some horrid disease from some stranger that had used the cups or slept in the bed. It did not matter to her that she could and would carry her own cups and bedding. The idea that someone she did not know had been in that room or eaten at that table caused her to flutter and call for her salts. However, Elizabeth knew that their grandfather Gardiner had died after contracting an illness on a journey, and therefore, her mother's worries were not beyond comprehension.

"She will likely only visit you when you are in town, and then there are so many things to distract her," Jane continued. "You must not let your fear of how vexatious Mr. Darcy finds her to keep you from accepting him."

Jane's arguments made sense. However, it was not just their mother who could be vexing.

"What of our sisters? Mama will expect us to help them find husbands."

Jane nodded. "And we will. Just think how helpful Mr. Darcy was in finding a husband for Miss Bingley."

Elizabeth could not help but laugh at the comment. It still surprised her that Mr. Darcy would participate in a scheme just to see his friend and Jane happy. Her lips curled up in that silly smile he so often caused her to smile. He had not just taken part in Miss Bingley's demise for Jane, he had done it for her – so that he might be free of all fetters to pursue her for his wife.

"I am certain Mama would not be pleased to have any of our sisters fall into marriage as Miss Bingley has," Elizabeth argued.

Jane giggled before countering, "And how many years has Mr. Darcy tolerated Miss Bingley as a friend even when she was so fixed on snaring him for herself?" She shook her head. "You are too fastidious. You cannot know every eventuality before it occurs. He has proven himself loyal and of good character. He loves you, and you love him, though you are too obstinate to admit it. Only good can come from such a match."

Elizabeth leaned back on the settee and looked up at the ceiling. "Am I capable of running so large a home?" she asked Jane without removing her eyes from plaster flowers and leaves that wound themselves around the edge of the room.

"Without a doubt," Jane replied quickly. "Mama has trained us well to run an estate twice the size of Longbourn, and you have the quickest mind of us all. You are perfectly capable of mastering whatever additional skills you might need."

She rolled her head to the side, so that she could see Jane. "Can I help guide a young lady like Miss Darcy?"

Jane smiled. "I think you can. You are forever instructing Lydia on one thing or another, and Miss Darcy seems a far more receptive pupil."

"But I know nothing of town," Elizabeth protested.

Jane turned and took her by the shoulders. "But you know everything about loving a sister. You are very good at it, even when she steals your bonnet and ruins your dress."

Elizabeth's brows furrowed, and her lips puckered. "Or when she is pushing you to admit what you know to be true."

Jane wrapped her arms around Elizabeth. "Do you admit it then? Do you love Mr. Darcy?"

Elizabeth drew a deep breath and expelled it to drive out the last worries and allow her confidence to fill in those places. "I do. I love Mr. Darcy. I believe I have for some time."

"Since he first insulted you." Jane pulled back and looked at her. "Do not shake your head. I am right as I usually am, though you will not admit it. If Mr. Goulding had said you were not handsome enough to tempt him, you would have laughed and made it a great joke. Do not deny it. I know it is true. But Mr. Darcy was different. You loved him from the moment you saw him."

"I could not love someone I did not know." Elizabeth extracted herself from her sister's embrace and rose. "I found him handsome. And anyone would feel the slight of a stranger far more greatly than that of a friend."

Jane laughed. "If you say so, but I think you are wrong."

Elizabeth rolled her eyes and shook her head.

"You will see," Jane said as she smoothed her skirt and straightened her sleeves. "I am right."

"You are not," Elizabeth muttered.

Jane's response was a smug smile which irritated Elizabeth more than any words might, and Jane knew it. It was how Jane always ended an argument when she thought she was right and Elizabeth was wrong.

"What book are you going to read?" Jane asked.

"I have not decided."

"Good, then, you can help me find a book before you do."

Sisters! Even the most understanding, proper, loving of sisters could be annoying, and yet, Elizabeth would not trade Jane for the world.

Chapter 13

Darcy nudged his horse to a faster pace. The day was young, and Rotten Row was occupied by several grooms exercising horses for their masters. A few well-dressed gentlemen dotted the trail here and there, but most men of Darcy's class were likely still in their beds. He smiled as he saw Bingley just ahead, and Sir Matthew just beyond him. He knew he would see at least one friend here at this hour. Seeing Sir Matthew would be a bonus. He would make a point of joining up with them soon.

"Darcy."

Darcy's lips curled into a partial snarl as he turned toward the unwelcome rider who had called to him. "Wickham. It seems a rather early hour for you to be out and about. I would expect you to still be abed, not that I expected you to be in town."

"Didn't expect me in Hertfordshire either, did you?" George Wickham teetered just a bit in his saddle. "I'm just on my way home to get some sleep," he added. "Not that I have not been in bed." A wolfish grin spread across Wickham's face.

"And what brings you to town?" Darcy asked, ignoring the implication of Wickham's words. The man was a profligate of the first order. That he had been keeping some woman company for most of the night was not a surprise.

"I am merely visiting some friends for a day or two," Wickham replied.

"I do hope you enjoy your visit." Darcy nudged his horse forward. He had no desire to remain here talking with Wickham. He did not care what the man was doing in town so long as he stayed with his own kind and did not attempt to visit at Darcy House.

Wickham did not, however, seem to be capable of letting Darcy depart with so short a conversation and moved his horse to keep pace with Darcy's.

"I hear you have guests."

Darcy glanced at him. "Do you?"

"I do. A whole house full of pretty ladies."

"And their father and mother," Darcy added. He

did not appreciate the suggestive tone Wickham was using.

"I also heard Miss Bennet is to marry your friend."

"She is." Darcy did not like the bent this conversation was taking. The knowledge of the Bennets being at Darcy House was easily explained away. Surely everyone in Hertfordshire knew Mrs. Bennet had been invited. However, the knowledge of Bingley's betrothal had only been shared with Mrs. Bennet after her arrival.

"I suppose you will wish to marry Miss Elizabeth eventually if you can convince her of your worth."

"Why would you say that?" Again, Darcy cast a wary glance at Wickham.

"Come now. We both know you fancy her. I saw how you looked at her when we met in Hertford-shire."

Darcy said nothing in the ensuing silence. He had suspected Wickham knew of his preference for Elizabeth. There was nothing to deny, but Darcy also did not wish to tell Wickham he was correct.

"It is too bad she has heard of your poor qualities. It might make it a great deal more challenging for you to persuade her to accept you."

Darcy wished to kick his horse into a gallop to be rid of the vermin next to him. "She is an intelligent young lady. I am certain she will soon discover your true talent is your deceitful tongue."

"You mean as your sister did?"

Darcy whirled toward him. "You will not mention my sister."

"Georgiana?" Wickham asked with a smile.

Darcy's eyes narrowed. "Yes," he ground out. "Your life depends upon it."

"Does it?"

Darcy wanted to wipe the smirk off Wickham's face with his fist. "My cousin does not make empty promises."

Wickham leaned close to Darcy. "How is the good colonel?" he whispered loudly.

Darcy drew back. The man positively reeked of alcohol. It was a wonder he could stay seated for he must be excessively foxed.

"He is well and staying at Darcy House. Would you care to give me your direction so that he might call on you?"

Wickham laughed and slapped Darcy's back.

"No, but I might call on him. It would be good to see Georgiana again. She's such a pretty thing, and Miss Lydia." He whistled. "Very agreeable and lively."

"You are not welcome to visit. Ever."

"Well, that would look right uncivilized of you to turn me away should I come to call on my friends the Bennets. I am certain that would curry you no favours. They already think you disagreeable."

"Go home."

The Bennets may have found him to be disagreeable at one time, but Darcy knew they now no longer did. There was very little fear that Wickham being turned away from Darcy House would do more than cause the youngest Bennet to be perturbed. However, Darcy knew that arguing with Wickham when he was sober was an act in futility, and it was even less productive when he was drunk.

"I may call," Wickham said as he turned his horse toward the park's exit.

"You will be turned away," Darcy replied.

Wickham's only response was to laugh loudly and wave.

"Who was that?" Bingley said as he and Sir Matthew approached Darcy.

Darcy closed his eyes. "Wickham."

"Wickham is in town?" Bingley asked in surprise.

Darcy nodded. "And threatening to call at Darcy House."

Bingley chuckled. "I would like to be there when he does, for I should like to witness the fond welcome he receives from Richard."

"He is not a friend?" Sir Matthew asked.

"He was. At one time," Darcy replied. "However, he has proven himself to be anything but a friend."

"Ah," Sir Matthew replied, "I shall ask no more."

"Thank you," said Darcy.

"Are you going to ride further?" Bingley asked.

Darcy shook his head. "No, I think I should go inform Richard of Wickham's presence."

Sir Matthew's brows rose.

"That man has damaged people close to us," Darcy said in explanation. "He narrowly escaped with his life the last time he and Richard met."

"Indeed?"

Darcy nodded. "If an innocent's reputation were

not at stake, I would tell you the tale, but as it is, I cannot."

"As I said, I will ask no more. I shall just remember that this Wickham is not to be trusted."

Wickham was most certainly not to be trusted, and that was the reason Darcy needed to speak to Richard and quite likely Mr. and Mrs. Bennet. He turned toward the exit of the park but then turned back to Bingley. "He mentioned that he knew you were getting married."

"He did?"

Darcy nodded.

"Gossip does circulate quickly," Bingley said with a sigh. "It is not so horrid to have it spread among your acquaintances when they are friends, but..."

Again, Darcy nodded. It was never pleasant when someone who was not friendly knew details about you that you did not wish for him to know. "He mentioned Elizabeth," Darcy added. "He knows I like her."

"Oh," Sir Matthew gasped, understanding dawning in his eyes. "This is that man? The one who has told lies about you and posed a danger to your lady and her sisters due to his debauchery?"

"Yes," Bingley replied.

They had told Sir Matthew some about Wickham after Sir Matthew had agreed to marry Caroline.

"Do you fear he can cause harm now?" Sir Matthew's mien was somber. It held no curiosity or amusement. He was, as he always seemed to be, sincere.

"I do not trust him to not act rashly," Darcy replied. "However, I do not expect him to be able to do them any harm while they are at Darcy House, for he shall not gain entrance."

Sir Matthew shook his head. "There are so many fools in this world, are there not?"

Neither Darcy nor Bingley could disagree with that.

"If you need anything," Sir Matthew continued, "do not hesitate to ask."

Darcy offered his thanks and set off for home.

Chapter 14

"Wickham is here? In town?" Richard's fork returned to his plate, still holding its piece of beef-steak.

"I admit I was surprised to see him and not pleasantly so."

Upon returning from his ride, Darcy had found his cousin eating breakfast and had chosen to join him and share his news since no one else was yet in the room.

Darcy took a sip of his coffee. "He knows Bingley is betrothed and that the Bennets are here as well as the fact that I like Elizabeth."

Richard's jaw tensed. "He has always been too good at ferreting out information," he muttered.

"Only when it serves his purpose," Darcy said after another sip of coffee.

Richard allowed it to be true.

Wickham was always attempting to gain information and then twisting it and turning it as needed to achieve his goals — whether that was getting himself out of trouble, placing Darcy in a precarious situation, or charming a young woman into thinking herself in love with him.

"However," Darcy continued. "That is not the worst of it."

"What could be worse?" Richard demanded.

"He said he might call." Darcy watched Richard's face darken. "He said it would be nice to see Georgiana again."

Richard muttered a curse as he shook his head. "Not while I still breath."

"I told him he would be turned away."

"Or worse," Richard muttered.

"Yes, I did tell him you were in residence. I hope it will help him be reasonable, but this is Wickham, and once he's set on an idea, there's little which can shake it from his head. This idea of his of calling here will likely be more firmly rooted in his mind than is normal since he sees this as a way to make certain the Bennets still view me as disagreeable."

"Have you instructed Abram that he is not to be admitted under any circumstances? Because doing harm to you is incentive enough for him to disregard any fear for his life that he should possess," Richard grumbled.

"I did. He will be turned away."

"Good." Richard shoved his beefsteak into his mouth and chewed with vigor as he stabbed another piece.

"Do not break the dishes," Darcy said with a smile. "I know you despise him, but please spare the plates."

Richard shook his head as he replied around his food. "If he were here, I'd not have to abuse your china."

"Then perhaps we will be fortunate, and the blackguard will call this afternoon."

Richard swallowed. "I almost hope we are."

"Good morning," Lydia chirped as she and Kitty entered the room. "Mary and Mama will be along soon, but Lizzy and Jane are likely still with Papa." She slid into a chair next to Richard. "You look a bit like a storm cloud, Colonel. Does he not, Kitty?"

"He does indeed!" Kitty agreed.

Darcy smiled at the exuberance of the two youngest Bennets. Perhaps, he would not need to fear Miss Lydia being put out if Wickham were turned away. He suspected that one word from *the colonel* would make all well in her eyes.

"We were just discussing some unpleasant business," Richard said in his own defense before popping another bite of food into his mouth.

"Well, you should not have been." Lydia poured a cup of tea and placed a roll on her plate. "It is not healthy. One should only think on happy things while eating, or one's stomach will ache dreadfully. And I imagine it becomes even more important to follow such a practice as one gets older. Old people seem to have so many ailments that if one can be prevented, it should be. Do you not think, Colonel?"

She smiled brightly at Richard as he attempted to clear his mouth of food before responding.

"Are you saying I am old?" he asked.

"Oh, goodness, no!" Lydia exclaimed. "Why would you think such a thing? Just because I mentioned your discussion of disagreeable things while eating and then the ailments of the elderly does not make you old." Her brows furrowed. "Does it?"

From her tone of voice, it sounded to Darcy as if

she had reasoned her way into doubting her own supposition.

"I'm not old," Richard replied.

"No, but you are older than I am." Lydia was still looking perplexed.

"That does not make me old. You are just young."

"Not so very young!" Lydia now sounded offended. She huffed and then shook her head as she sat straighter and lifted her chin. "We must think on pleasant things," she instructed. "Dash can hold a biscuit on his nose until I tell him he can eat it."

Darcy chuckled at Richard's look of bewilderment caused by the sudden change of topics.

"He will sit just so." Lydia held her finger on her nose as if it was a biscuit. "And then when I say 'good boy,' he flicks it in the air and catches it." She spooned some jam onto her bun. "He is very smart."

"And adorable," Kitty added. "You should have seen him wearing his cravat last night. I tried to draw it, but he is not very good at sitting still just yet."

"Except for when he has a biscuit that is on his nose," Richard inserted.

"Yes, but he cannot sit forever with it on his nose. Half a minute is all. Longer than that would be torturous. He is just a puppy," Lydia's tone held a great deal of shock.

"But perhaps he could learn to sit with it longer," Kitty said.

Lydia tipped her head to one side and then the other. "Perhaps, he could." She took a bite of her bun.

"Do you think we will get to purchase some ribbons today?" she asked Kitty. "I should like one for my bonnet. Red would be delightful to go with my sprigged muslin dress, do you not think so, Colonel?"

Richard, who had just taken a sip of his tea, coughed. "I really could not say," he managed after a few moments of coughing followed by another sip of tea. "I am not even sure I know what sprigged muslin is."

"It is the one I wore when we had our dance lesson." Lydia's lashes fluttered as she blinked.

It was as if she could not fathom that the colonel did not know to which dress she referred. She might be the Bennet who posed to cause the most disturbance to Darcy's life, but Lydia was also proving to be the most entertaining, and, surprisingly, he was beginning to appreciate her lively mind. Lively, but not logical. He chuckled to himself behind his cup.

"Maria Lucas has always said a red ribbon would set it off nicely," Lydia added.

She said it in such a tone that Darcy could imagine her mother saying that very thing. Lydia was indeed her mother's daughter. He had to admit he was enjoying the chance to learn so many intimate details about Elizabeth's family. He shook his head before taking another sip of his coffee. He never thought he would be enjoying having the Bennets at Darcy House. He had thought he could endure them, but he had not expected to benefit from their stay in such a fashion.

"Well, then it must be true," Richard replied.

Richard did know how to bow out of an argument he was sure to lose.

Lydia huffed as she swallowed the bite of jam covered bun she had taken. "I shall wear it again tomorrow, and you will see."

Darcy chuckled to himself. Richard was not

going to get away from the argument without admitting defeat. Miss Lydia was a determined young woman.

"I look forward to being proven wrong," Richard responded with a smile that was returned in kind.

And his cousin, who would have at any other time likely argued his position of not needing to know which dress Georgiana wore or with what ribbon, was in danger of becoming the pupil rather than the instructor.

Chapter 15

Elizabeth rolled her shoulders and rubbed her neck. The rest had felt good, but the stiffness that followed was not as pleasant.

"That is not the best place to take a nap," said her father. "Those chairs were not designed for comfort when resting."

Elizabeth smiled. The soreness in her neck could attest to the truth of his word. "How are you feeling?"

"As well as a man who is confined to a room might," he replied with a smirk. "Truly, the pain is not so bad today as it was yesterday. I do believe in another week's time I will be set to return to my study, unless?" His brows rose and then waggled.

"Unless what?" she asked.

"Unless more time is needed at Darcy House?"

Jane laughed from her place near the window

where she was keeping a watch on the front door of Darcy House. Elizabeth knew that her sister was hoping for Mr. Bingley to call again today.

"For either of you," her father added.

"I believe Mr. Bingley intends to return to Hertfordshire," Jane replied.

"But will he bring his friend?" Mr. Bennet asked.

"I doubt he could keep his friend from following him."

Jane's answer was met with a chuckle from Mr. Bennet.

"What think you of this, Lizzy?" her father asked. "I have not inquired about your opinion of Mr. Darcy since before taking up residence in this room. I should think I — and that rascal of a dog — have given you enough time to consider all that might need considering. Ah! I am right, am I not? That is why your sister is looking as if she is about to burst, is it not, Lizzy?"

Elizabeth's cheeks grew warm. "Yes."

He clapped his hands. "Does your mother know?"

Elizabeth shook her head. "Only Jane."

"Not Mr. Darcy?" her father asked in surprise.

Again, Elizabeth shook her head.

"But you would be favourable to an offer of marriage from the man?"

Light as a butterfly landing upon a rose in the garden at Longbourn, nerves alighted in Elizabeth's chest. Below the lace trimmed edge of her day gown, her heart raced. There was a slight uneasiness to the feeling but not so unsettling as it had been before she had come to her decision while talking to Jane yesterday. It was becoming a familiar, nearly welcomed, excitement of her senses very like unto how she felt when Mr. Darcy said something about loving her but heightened by the knowledge that she returned his sentiments.

"I would be." She knew that the foolish smile, which accompanied any sweet words from Mr. Darcy, was now scrawled across her face.

"Your mother will be in her glory."

Elizabeth was not sure she had ever seen her father smile so broadly. To her, it looked a lot like her father was in his glory as much as her mother might be on hearing such a thing, though her father displayed his delight in a more subdued fashion.

"To return to Longbourn with two daughters so well-matched," he continued, "she will be the envy of the community. Well, of the ladies of the community that is." He chuckled and then expelled a breath. "Do you think we can find three more such gents before my leg heals? I can insist that the physician recommends I not be moved for longer if necessary."

"Papa!" cried Jane. "You sound more like Mama than yourself."

He only chuckled in response. "Your mother is not your only parent who has worried about your futures."

"Indeed?" The comment surprised Elizabeth. Her father had never appeared to her to be overly concerned with anything beyond the here and now.

"Oh, it is very true. I would do almost anything for any of girls. I cannot say I look forward to parting with any of you, but it is not so dreadful to contemplate when I know you will be cared for so well."

He chuckled again. "I guess your mother and I have begun to prove the naysayers wrong," he murmured.

Jane and Elizabeth shared a confused look.

"What naysayers, Papa?" Jane asked.

He shrugged and smoothed his blanket. "I did not marry a gentleman's daughter."

Jane and Elizabeth waited patiently as her father found it necessary to smooth the same portion of his bedding before continuing.

"I had relations who condemned me for lowering myself so." He shrugged again. "Fanny Gardiner had more ability to run an estate than the young ladies of my circle. She was not the most intellectual of the lot of ladies, but she knew how to manage things and," he smiled at some imaginary object far in the distance, "she was prettier than any lady I had ever seen before or indeed have ever seen since. Save for my daughters, but then they all resemble their mother."

Elizabeth had never heard her father speak in such an affectionate way about their mother. She had always known he loved Mama, but he had never said so much in praise of her. He often teased about her beauty being enticing to others, but at this moment, there was no teasing tone. His words were spoken in such a sincere and almost longing fashion that Elizabeth could not help but to feel them greatly.

In addition to this new realization of how deeply

her father loved her mother, Elizabeth realized that she had never considered how he might have been looked upon for marrying the daughter of a country solicitor. She, herself, had never felt a compelling need to make a great divide between classes, but then that was likely because she had relations in trade.

"Mr. Collins offering for you, Lizzy," her father's words interrupted her contemplations, "was indeed a thing of significance as your mother was never accepted by his father. So, to have his son accept the daughter of my unacceptable wife was a true gesture of goodwill." He shook his head. "Not that he would ever be good enough for any of you in my eyes. He has too much of his father's preposterousness. Not even Lydia, who I must say has the most creative way of reasoning out anything, would be well-suited to such foolishness.

"There were others as well. It is not easy to move from one sphere to another without someone watching and waiting for you to fail."

A whoosh of air from Elizabeth was met with a shake of her father's head.

"You will do well, as will Jane, and, I hope, eventually Mary, Kitty, and Lydia will follow suit." He smiled. "Perhaps we should stay longer so that the colonel has more time to instruct Lydia."

Elizabeth and Jane laughed.

"I appreciate your willingness to see me entertained, but there is a gentleman below who would surely like a few hours of Lizzy's time, and there is also an outing planned. I would not wish to keep you both from such things." He winked and picked up his book.

"I have my bell," he said when they did not immediately rise. "If I have need of anything, I shall summons someone. Now, away with you." He made a sweeping motion with his hand in the direction of the door. "I will be well."

"There is nothing you need?" Jane asked as she rose from her chair.

"Nothing, save a kiss for each of my cheeks," he replied, tapping his left cheek for Jane to kiss and then doing the same to his right for Elizabeth before settling into the silence of the room when the door clicked closed.

Chapter 16

Elizabeth wandered the hall from the sitting room almost to the door of Mr. Darcy's study and back three times before finding enough courage to rap softly at his door. She blew out a breath and was just about to scurry away, assuming he had not heard her knock when the door before her opened.

"Miss Elizabeth."

Darcy's smile of greeting was enough to cause her heart to flutter. It was intoxicating to be met with such pleasure.

"Please, come in," he offered.

"We are to leave shortly," she said as she entered at his invitation. "My father has insisted that he be left alone and that Jane and I go with Mama and the others."

She looked around the room as she was talking. It was not much larger than Papa's study at Longbourn, but it was much more organized. Books did not lie upon shelves. They stood in fine array. Papers were not scattered across the desk but were contained within tidy piles. The room seemed to exemplify the personality of its master – dignified, reserved, and proper.

She took a seat in the one chair that faced the door but was positioned in such a way that its occupant could share in the conversation at the hearth to their right or with Mr. Darcy while he sat at his desk on the left. It was a plush chair with a wide seat of creamy fabric decorated with flowers and vines.

She smoothed her skirt and looked up to see Darcy staring at her.

"Am I not supposed to sit here?" She made to move.

"No. Stay as you are. You are so charmingly arranged." He shook his head. "I am quite overcome with how charming you look there."

Could cheeks burst into flames? If they could, Elizabeth was certain hers were very close to igniting from the pleasure in the tone of his voice and the intensity of the look in his eyes. It was perhaps best if she did not come to his study in the future. It felt far too dangerous a place to be.

"You are going shopping?"

Mr. Darcy moved around his desk and took his place behind it which made Elizabeth feel only slightly better as now she was separated from him by a substantial piece of furniture, yet he looked so... She could not describe it beyond the thought that the position fit him. He filled the chair with such authority and confidence that it was nearly palpable. It was no wonder Mr. Bingley gave such weight to any of Mr. Darcy's advice. How did one not listen to this man?

"I am," she replied when she had found her voice.

He seemed at a loss for how to continue the conversation, so she added, "I am not a lover of shopping as much as my mother or Lydia, but I must say I am eager to view the world in this part of London."

"Have you not shopped in town before?"

She smiled at his surprise. It was understandable. She had visited London many times to visit her aunt and uncle, and Mr. Darcy was well-aware of that fact. "I have, but we have never ventured to Bond Street."

"Never?" His surprise had not receded.

"Never," she assured him. "My uncle has many connections, but I am not certain if they extend to Bond Street. But whether they do or not, we have always frequented shops nearer to his home. Travel time is always a consideration for my aunt. She does have young ones at home, and though she employs a nursemaid, she does not like to be completely absent from their lives."

He seemed to relax into his chair at her words. She knew he liked both her aunt and uncle Gardiner greatly.

"I can understand such a sentiment. My mother insisted on not being parted from me for an overlong period of time when I was young."

He wore a soft smile as he spoke.

"Georgiana does not remember, but our mother was the same with her until she became too ill to leave her room." He sighed.

"Did you visit her then?" Elizabeth could not begin to imagine the sorrow that having a gravely ill parent would bring to a child no matter how young or old he was.

He nodded. "We did."

"That must have given her great joy," Elizabeth said softly.

He nodded once again but did not speak. How she would like to ask him more about his mother, but she dared not, for she did not know how best to approach such a thing. Her mother refused to speak of her father or mother and had scolded anytime Elizabeth had made a curious inquiry. So, to press the topic felt wrong even if it was not.

Darcy's eyes focused back on her. "I should like to tell you about her sometime."

"I would like that. Very much."

Lydia and Kitty scurried past the open door.

"It looks as if it is nearly time for you to depart."

Elizabeth sighed. As much as she longed to see the people and the shops on Bond Street, she also wished to remain here with him. Her heart and mind seemed a jumble of opposing feelings lately as it tried to decide where it belonged and how it fit in that place.

He rose from his seat and coming around his desk once again, extended his hand to her. "I shall see you off." His lips tipped up on one side. "I realize you must go fetch your things, but I will wait for you and see you to the carriage. I almost wish I was going, so that I could walk about with you on my arm." He wrapped her arm around his. "Maybe one day we will stroll down Bond Street together, and we can even visit one of the auction houses to select a few things for the house."

He was doing it again – speaking as if they were partners in life, as if this were already her home, and as if he valued her opinion and input. And she was wearing that silly grin that accompanied such things. However, this time instead of saying nothing. She smiled up at him and said, "I do hope so."

He stopped short of exiting the room and turned hopeful, yet uncertain, eyes toward her.

She shrugged. "There might be a thing or two that the house could use." Her heart beat wildly at such a proclamation of her affections.

A smile, large, bright, and filled with pleasure, spread slowly across his face. "Do you mean it?"

"I try not to tell falsehoods, Mr. Darcy." She arched a brow impertinently and attempted to ignore the heat which flooded her cheeks. "I should very much like to go shopping with you."

"Just shopping?" His eyes sparkled with merriment.

She shrugged one shoulder. "That is all you have asked me to do, is it not?"

He opened his mouth to speak, but at that moment, a tan and black blur raced into the room and between them.

"Dash!" Georgiana called as she hurried in behind him.

Elizabeth heard Darcy sigh as he turned toward the pup, who was standing on one of the chairs before the hearth. "Always Richard's chair," he muttered. Then, he looked at her. "Shall we discuss more than shopping later?"

"Yes, Mr. Darcy," she replied as her heart skittered and skipped, "I think we should."

Chapter 17

Inside the cobbler's shop, Elizabeth stood near where Georgiana sat trying on the lovely burgundy silk slippers which had been made for her.

"What do you think?" Georgiana asked, holding out her foot and tipping it this way and that for everyone to admire.

"I could dance for hours in those!" Lydia declared.

"They are beautiful," Elizabeth said.

"Are they comfortable?" Mrs. Annesley asked. "Is the fit good?"

"Oh, yes," inserted Mrs. Bennet. "Pretty shoes are only wonderful if they do not cause sores."

"Stand and give them a try," the shopkeeper encouraged as he stood back and hooked his thumbs on his apron. "My slippers are of the finest quality, as you know. I am certain they will not cause any discomfort." He stood in front of a counter that was piled with leather, fabric, and forms. Behind the counter was a workbench with several partially finished boots and shoes on it.

As Georgiana stood, Lydia took her hands and led her in a few patterns of the dance they had practiced in the ballroom with Mr. Hughes. "Did they make you feel like you could complete that dance over and over?" Lydia asked when she finally released Georgiana's hands. "You performed the figures very well."

Elizabeth shook her head. Lydia had so much confidence. There never seemed to be a situation in which she found herself that caused her to pause and watch warily. No, Lydia threw herself most happily into any fun scheme that presented itself. It was an admirable quality in some ways, for it meant that she was not held back from experiencing new and delightful things by fear. However, it also meant that sometimes she found herself in less than desirable places because she had not first carefully considered where a plan might end. Thankfully, as of yet, none of those scrapes had caused anything more than a few moments of unease for her and her sisters.

"They are absolutely perfect!" Georgiana declared. "I only wish I could keep them on my feet now."

"Oh, you mustn't," chided Lydia. "The streets would see them destroyed before we got to the carriage."

Georgiana giggled. "You could carry me."

"What is the use of a pair of shoes if one cannot walk when wearing them?" muttered Mary.

"She can walk," Kitty shot a displeased look at her sister, "just not on the streets. Slippers are not for out of doors. Everybody knows that." Kitty drew out the word everybody and rolled her eyes as she said it.

"Girls," Mrs. Bennet said sternly.

Elizabeth shared a questioning look with Jane. Their mother rarely scolded in public. In fact, had they been in a shop in Meryton, she might have taken up Kitty's position in reprimand of Mary.

Thankfully, none of Elizabeth's sisters continued the argument, and Miss Darcy was allowed to remove her new slippers and put on her boots while the shopkeeper wrapped up the precious new footwear, which was then handed to the footman who accompanied them.

Elizabeth linked arms with Jane as they made their way among and around the people on the street to another shop not far away. She was glad that she had Jane to guide her, so that she could pay attention to the people they passed as well as to the shop fronts rather than attending carefully to whether they were still following Miss Darcy.

Walking this street on the arm of Mr. Darcy would indeed be delightful. She made a mental note of where particular stores of interest were, so she could mention them to him when next they spoke. It was not that she wished to purchase anything inside of them, it was just that the glimpse through an open door or window was enough to arouse her curiosity.

Her attention turned back to her party as she stepped into a store that sold cases and cases of accessories. Everything was displayed so well, and Elizabeth delighted in watching the various clerks assisting the customers.

"Fanny Gardiner!" Some woman's high-pitched declaration pierced through the din of the store. "I would never have imagined that I would see you here, in this district of town, and yet, here you are."

"Are you well?" Jane whispered to their mother who had frozen and paled. "Mama?"

"Yes, yes. I am well," Mrs. Bennet assured her, but Elizabeth was not convinced she was speaking the truth.

Mrs. Bennet turned to greet the lady who had crossed from where she had been standing at a case to where the Bennet party was.

"It is Mrs. Bennet now." Mrs. Bennet extended her hand to the lady. "I am sorry. I would greet you properly, but I do not know your name. I am sure it is no longer Miss Foster."

Elizabeth watched the exchange of greeting curiously. Her mother's chin was lifted, and her back was straight and stiff. As far as she could remember, Elizabeth had seen her mother assume such a posture only once before when Mrs. Long had said something disparaging about Jane three years ago.

"Indeed, it is not," the woman said with a laugh. "It is Mrs. Salter now."

"Mrs. Salter, it is a surprise to see you after all these years." Mrs. Bennet motioned for Jane to step forward. "Allow me to introduce you to my daughters."

She waited until the woman before her nodded and motioned for her to continue.

"This is my eldest, Jane. Next to her is Elizabeth, and then Mary. Kitty and Lydia are examining the gloves with our friend Miss Darcy." She motioned to where Georgiana was pulling on a pair of calf-skin gloves while Lydia praised them profusely.

"Five daughters?" Mrs. Salter asked.

"Yes."

"Are these all your children then?" The woman continued to look amused by that fact for some reason.

"Yes."

To Elizabeth, it seemed strange that her mother would not inquire as to Mrs. Salter's children. In fact, it was very unusual for her mother to be so silent.

"I do hope your husband's estate is not entailed – he does have an estate, does he not?"

"As you well know, my husband's estate is Long-bourn in Hertfordshire, and it is entailed, which you also know."

The woman fiddled with her gloves. "Oh, I had forgotten. It has been what?" She looked at Jane. "Twenty-three years since we last saw each other."

Mrs. Bennet said nothing in reply, but her cheeks turned from their pale colour to a rosy hue.

"I have two sons – an heir and a spare – as they say," Mrs. Salter said with a laugh. "And one daughter. She is in her second season, but we do have some high hopes that there will be some very happy news for her soon." She lifted her chin as she smiled down at first Mrs. Bennet and then Jane, Elizabeth, and Mary. "I mustn't keep you from your friend – Miss Darcy, did you say it was?"

"Yes," Elizabeth pressed her lips together. It was not for her to answer such a question, but this woman was so gratingly arrogant in that overly pleasant fashion of some catty women that for a moment she forgot herself.

"Well, I see you are still able to worm your way up from your position into one that is higher, but then you were always overreaching your bounds, were you not, Fanny?"

Elizabeth's eyes grew wide both at the accusation and the cold turn of the woman's tone.

"He preferred me," Mrs. Bennet's response was spoken softly. "He still does."

Mrs. Salter smiled tightly. "Yes, well, be that as it may, although that got him what he wanted in the moment, it did not get him what he needed, now, did it?" Again, she looked at Jane.

"I assure you we are perfectly happy with the children the Lord saw fit to give us."

The woman shrugged and sighed as she affected a look of nonchalance. "Such beautiful daughters," she said. "Daughters," she repeated. "It almost makes you wonder if it is not punishment for an indiscretion."

Elizabeth caught her jaw before her mouth dropped open.

"And your daughters seem to have learned well from you," the venomous viper of a woman continued. "I hear one of them caused quite a scandal at a ball recently, but I digress." She waved her words away as if shooing away a servant. "It has been delightful to see you again after all these years. I shall have to tell our friends. They will be overcome with the surprise just as I was when I saw you enter this store." She turned to leave, but Mrs. Bennet's words stopped her.

"Do try to tell them the truth this time. Unlike you did all those years ago."

"I am afraid I do not understand your meaning."

Elizabeth could tell from the way Mrs. Salter's

lashes fluttered that she knew precisely of what Mrs. Bennet was speaking.

"Jane, dear," said their mother. "When is your birthday?"

"May 24," Jane replied.

"Just three days before my anniversary," Mrs. Bennet added.

"That does not mean you did not...well, we will not speak of such thing in public. It is not how the well-bred do things."

"No, they prefer to gossip behind closed doors," Mary muttered. "One is so much better than the other," she added, her tone dripping with sarcasm.

Mrs. Salter gasped. "Such talk! You will do well to see any of your daughters well-matched with such behavior."

"Are you not happy it is not your problem then?" Mrs. Bennet replied with a smirk. "They all take after their father in some way. Mary has her father's love of the sardonic while Lizzy has his wit and teasing nature. Jane has his kind heart, Kitty has his willingness to please those she loves, and Lydia has his determined spirit. If you cannot admire those things in my daughters, then I do not see how you could have ever truly admired their father. But then, you did not. You just did not wish for him to admire me." She turned to her daughters. "Come along. We should not keep our friend waiting." She cast a glance at Mrs. Salter. "It would be rude." Then with a flick of her head that would rival Lydia's best performance, she led Jane, Mary, and Elizabeth away from Mrs. Salter.

Chapter 18

"But Mama, I really must get a red ribbon," Lydia protested upon hearing Mrs. Bennet's suggestion of returning to Darcy House without entering any other shops.

Mrs. Bennet pursed her lips, furrowed her brow, blew out a breath, and gave a small shrug. "One ribbon?" Her tone was filled with uncertainty.

It was not like their mother to be so brief when shopping, nor was it like her to question Lydia's wants. On most occasions, Lydia had only to hint that she might like this or that, and it was secured if at all possible.

"We could wait for her in the carriage," Elizabeth suggested softly to her mother. "She will be well with Jane and Mrs. Annesley to attend her."

"But that woman – oh, it is too much," Mrs. Bennet dug in her reticule and pulled out her salts. "I do not wish to see her again."

"Nor do I," Elizabeth agreed. "She is most horrid." She placed an arm around her mother's shoulders. "In fact," she said in a whisper, "she is so horrid that she makes Miss Bingley and Mrs. Long look rather pleasant."

Her words did what they were intended to do by causing Mrs. Bennet to giggle. The sound made Elizabeth's heart ache a bit less. While it had pained her to hear that woman speak so cruelly to her mother, the worst of it was how it discomposed her mother. A giggle meant that her mother's usual vigor and cheerfulness would soon be restored.

"She does, does she not?" Mrs. Bennet took one more whiff of her salts before tucking them back in her reticule.

"One more shop," she said to Lydia with a smile. "I think I can endure one more shop."

"I dare say Mrs. Salter will not approach you again," Jane said as they began moving toward the street.

Mrs. Bennet sighed. "Perhaps not today, but..." She shook her head. "She is not the sort to be easily put off. She tormented me for months."

"How do you know her?" Elizabeth held one of her mother's arms while Jane had the other.

"I went to school. It was not a fancy school. It was a good one, but not the sort that Miss Darcy would have attended, I suppose. Your aunt Phillips and I were sent to polish a few skills which might help us rise above our beginnings. I managed it. My sister did not, but then I have always been more accomplished at the skills necessary to manage a home, and, well, not to be too very arrogant, I have always been the prettier of us two. You know your aunt well, and I am sure you can see the truth in what I am saying."

Elizabeth had to admit that if she were to compare her aunt Phillips and her mother only on beauty, her mother was most decidedly the prettier sister, and, if she were to pause and consider the soirees held at her aunt's home and compare them to what was had at Longbourn, she would also have to admit that her mother was indeed more skilled than her aunt Phillips at entertaining. However, until this moment, she had never stopped to ponder such things. Her mother had always just been her mother and her aunt, her aunt. She had not thought about them as sisters who might compete with each other or as young women learning skills and hoping to make a good match. Elizabeth wondered if when she had a daughter, she would also be viewed as just Mother and nothing else?

"Mrs. Salter is from Hertfordshire, or she was. Her family has since moved to smaller accommodations." Mrs. Bennet looked around her and lowered her voice. "They had to cut expenses, you see. Her father liked to gamble, and he was a very poor player." She raised her eyebrows and gave her daughters a look that spoke of how absolutely dreadful such a thing was.

"But if Mrs. Salter was from Hertfordshire, how did you not meet her until you were at school?" Jane asked what Elizabeth was also thinking.

"Oh, I did not say I met her there," Mrs. Bennet said with a laugh.

"Did you not?" Elizabeth queried. Had her mother not answered the question of how she knew Mrs. Salter with the information that she had gone to school?

"No, I simply was beginning my tale. I knew Mrs. Salter for years. She was always a jackanapes." Here she paused to shake her head and cluck.

"Always thinking so highly of herself. Oh, my, the airs she put on."

"So, you were not friends?" Jane asked.

"Goodness! Never! I was polite to her because my father needed me to be welcoming to all. His business was only profitable if he was sought after, and one will not seek out a solicitor whose daughters are rude."

"I see," Elizabeth muttered, again being struck by how she had never truly considered what her mother's life might have been like as a young girl.

"Well," Mrs. Bennet continued, "when Mrs. Salter – Miss Foster then – turned sixteen, she took a liking for the young gentleman at Longbourn." She sighed. "He was a handsome fellow, and he still is." She winked at Elizabeth. "A little older but no less handsome."

Elizabeth could not help but smile at her mother's comments and be reminded of how her father had spoken so lovingly of her mother earlier that day. There was no doubting what she and her sisters had always known – despite their differences, eccentricities, teasing, and nagging, their parents loved each other.

"Miss Foster, who is a year older than I, was at

the same school I attended, and she attempted to outdo me in most things, which in some areas was not so great a task. I shall never be an accomplished musician, for instance. But there were areas where, try as she might, she could not earn the praise I did, and to make matters worse, the young man she wished to have call on her, showed a preference for me."

That part, Elizabeth had guessed from the conversation between Mama and Mrs. Salter.

"Oh, this shop is delightful!" Mrs. Bennet cried. She followed behind Lydia and exclaimed over this ribbon or that lace. "And the caps!"

"Will you get one, Mama?" Kitty asked. "That one right there with the rosette. Would not that look divine on you?"

"To be sure!"

Elizabeth knew that the cap was purchased even before her mother asked the shop assistant to wrap it up.

"You should buy some lace, Lizzy," said Mrs. Bennet. "You see Jane is already looking at a fine lot of it there. You may need it if you ever decide to accept Mr. Darcy. I do not know what keeps you from bringing him up to scratch. He is the finest gentleman I have ever met. Well, aside from Mr. Bingley, of course. And your father. And Colonel Fitzwilliam – he is such a nice gentleman, is he not? And a colonel, too." Her brow furrowed. "Sir Matthew is lovely as well from what I could tell. I am not certain why he would wish to marry Miss Bingley, but then I am not well-acquainted with how they get on."

"You did not like Mr. Darcy," Elizabeth reminded her mother.

"With good reason! He was rude. One of my daughters, not handsome enough? I knew it could not be true. Anyone with eyes can see that my daughters are amongst the fairest in the kingdom." She pulled out a bit of lace and held it up for Elizabeth. "This will be perfect." Then she turned to the shop attendant and had it wrapped up without waiting for Elizabeth to agree or disagree.

"Mr. Darcy is very clever, though. He soon realized his error."

"Yes, he finds Lizzy more than handsome now," Jane teased with a smile, causing Elizabeth to blush. However, she did not refute the statement, for she knew it was true.

"Well, now, if Lydia would just select what she

needs," Mrs. Bennet flitted off to give her assistance to her youngest.

A short argument about the correct shade of red as well as the width that would be best broke out as was often the case when Lydia and their mother clashed over something. However, it ended as it always did — and in short order — with Mrs. Bennet purchasing both items and telling Lydia how she would see that her mother was right when they returned home.

"They are very alike, are they not?" Elizabeth asked Jane, who nodded her agreement.

"Ah!" Mrs. Bennet's sigh as they stepped out of the shop was one of relief. "We can now go home having had a most successful outing," she declared.

And they did.

Chapter 19

Darcy stretched and rose from his chair. He had slipped back into his study after tea and before dinner to complete some instructions that he wished to send off to his solicitor just as soon as he had secured Elizabeth's acceptance of his offer... he smiled... which he would make either this evening should he find the correct moment or tomorrow when he would ask her to take a drive with him in the park.

Her father had already given Darcy permission to make his offer. They had discussed many particulars about marriage settlements and the like while playing a game of chess when the ladies had been out shopping. Mr. Bennet was turning out to be a gentleman who Darcy not only liked but could also admire. The man was sharp and an excessively good chess player. Darcy had yet to win a game.

"I do not know how you will ever choose." Bingley's tone was teasing as he entered Darcy's study behind Richard.

"I shall just see which one she seems to favour, and if I wish for the discussion to stop, I will pick that one. However, if I fancy a bit of a row, I shall then pick the other."

"With whom are you considering starting an argument?" Darcy asked.

"Miss Lydia," Bingley replied. "Apparently, she has decided to wear her muslin to dinner instead of waiting until tomorrow, even if it is more of a day dress than a dinner dress. She just will not be able to sleep if she does not know which red ribbon the colonel prefers. He is the expert in all things red, you see."

Darcy chuckled. "Is he? I did not know."

"It's on account of his uniform," Bingley added. Then, he sat primly on the edge of his seat, clasped his hands on his knees, and batted his lashes as he said, "It's red, you know."

Richard cuffed Bingley on the shoulder. "It is red," he defended. "Miss Lydia is just enamoured with all things uniform. It is not so strange a thing." He smiled as he slipped into his normal seat before the hearth. "And I do cut a fine figure, so you really cannot blame a young woman for being duly impressed."

Bingley dissolved into laughter.

"I must have missed an important discussion," Darcy said with a laugh as he leaned against his desk.

"Oh, it was entertaining," Richard agreed. "Miss Lydia and Mrs. Bennet hold differing opinions on which of the red ribbons they purchased today will look best with Miss Lydia's muslin. You know, the one she mentioned this morning?"

"I do remember that conversation."

"Miss Kitty is certain Miss Lydia is correct while Miss Mary thinks that a ribbon is a ribbon, and it is foolish to be arguing over something so trivial." Bingley tipped his head and waggled his eyebrows as he smirked.

"And that did not sit well with either Miss Lydia or Miss Kitty, I suppose," Darcy said.

"Oh, most certainly not!" said Richard. "They were still discussing the issue when they went up to dress for dinner." He sighed. "We are assured of at least thirty minutes of silence on the topic of ribbons."

Darcy tipped his head and studied his cousin. Richard did not look as put out with the topic of ribbons as his voice seemed to convey. "You could avoid all of this if you returned to Matlock House."

Richard shook his head. "I have to return to my men the day after tomorrow. There are drills scheduled." He reclined in his chair and crossed his ankles. "We may be shipped off soon."

"To the continent?" Darcy asked in surprise. Richard had said nothing of his unit being called up.

"Nothing is certain just yet, but the whispers I heard today were that it could happen." He shrugged. "There is also more talk of unrest at the mills, and Father expects it to get worse before it gets better. So, I could be sent in that direction as well – which is what Mother prefers." He smiled wryly. "She has made her preference known to Father, of course."

"You do not know?"

Richard shook his head in response to his cousin's inquiry. "Not at present." He drew in a deep breath and blew it out slowly through his nose. "You'll have to see to the betterment of Miss Lydia without me."

"I shall do my best," Darcy assured him. "And Bingley can help me once we return to Netherfield."

"I will stand at your side and say yay and nay as instructed," said Bingley. "But I fear I am not the best at directing young ladies. You have met my youngest sister, have you not?"

All three of them chuckled at the thought. Caroline Bingley followed her own path without anyone diverting her from her desired purpose. Well, Darcy amended, that is she had always proceeded in such a fashion until recently.

"Perhaps we should have Sir Matthew join our efforts," Darcy suggested.

Bingley shook his head. "He is busy enough directing my sister. I should not like to tax him with anything else after he has so graciously taken her off my hands." He shook his head again but this time with an air of bewilderment. "Have I told you that Hurst claims she seems happy?"

"So soon?" asked Richard. "The man works quickly."

"It seems he does," said Bingley as he nodded his head. "She has been humming as she works on her stitching, and Hurst has seen her smiling for no reason and looking out the window for moments at a time."

"You must be pleased," said Darcy. He knew that his friend had always hoped that both of his sisters would be happily matched.

"I am."

The room fell into silence for a few moments.

"I spoke to Father about the possibility of resigning my commission."

Darcy's brows rose. Richard had always claimed he would be a military man until he died. He even scoffed at men who had retired from their positions earlier than age and mobility required.

"Might I inquire about why you are considering such a thing?" Darcy asked.

Richard shrugged and again expelled a great breath through his nose. "You may as well. Father did."

"And?" Darcy prodded.

"Georgiana will be out next year. You will be married, and who knows if you will be able to see to her as you ought."

"I am certain I shall be able to care for both her and my wife."

"There is no need to be affronted," Richard said

with a smile. "What if your wife is pregnant with your heir? It is possible."

Darcy rubbed the back of his neck. He had not thought about that scenario. The left side of his lips tipped up in a half smile. It was not that he had not thought about his wife being pregnant. No, he had considered that aspect of marrying. He had just never considered that it might interfere with Georgiana's season.

"Your mother could see to her," Darcy argued.

"Mother?" Richard shook his head. "She would have her married off within a fortnight."

Darcy laughed. "She would not. But I do understand your meaning. She does like to make matches."

"Which is why I should be on home soil to stand next to Georgiana when needed."

"There is no other reason?" Darcy asked.

"None," Richard said.

However, Darcy noted that his cousin's eyes did not lift from their study of the tips of the boots on his outstretched feet and there was a slight reddening of Richard's ears. Both were signs that Richard was not being straightforward.

"You'll likely need help with one or another of the Bennet sisters as well," Richard added.

Ah, now to Darcy, that sounded as if they were getting closer to the heart of the matter.

"Their mother will wish for them to be presented at some point, and it will not do for them to cause a stir. Your wife and Mrs. Bingley will be in the process of adjusting to their new environment. I would not wish for either of them to be censured for one of their sisters."

"That would be unfortunate," Darcy agreed. It was not completely unlikely that such an event could happen, but he highly doubted that it was the reason Richard truly wished to help with the younger Bennet's presentation to London society.

"And they will be relations of Georgiana's, so we must consider the impact of such a thing on her as well."

And they were very neatly and safely back to Georgiana. Darcy smiled. "I do hope your father discovers a way for you to keep your uniform and still be able to squire around Georgiana and the Miss Bennets, for I am certain at least one of the Miss Bennets would be more inclined to listen to you when you are in uniform than if you were not."

Bingley laughed. "Indeed. Her red ribbon would be for naught if there were not a uniform at her side to compliment it."

"The ribbon is to match her dress," Richard argued. "She did not buy it to match my uniform."

"If you say so," said Bingley rising from his chair. "Shall we return to the drawing room to await the ladies and our dinner?"

Darcy motioned toward the door.

"She did not buy it for me," Richard said once again.

"No?" Bingley replied. "Then why does she require your opinion and not mine?"

"Because I have better taste," said Richard.

Darcy shook his head and followed his cousin and friend from the room. He would have to take note of how Miss Lydia and Richard interacted tonight if he could keep his eyes off Elizabeth long enough to do so.

Chapter 20

In the drawing room, tables were being arranged for a game of cards. Lydia was directing the proceeding, but only with the approval of the colonel. Had Richard not picked Lydia's choice of ribbon, his consent might not be so eagerly sought after now. However, he had chosen Lydia's ribbon, and now found himself deferred to on most things since he obviously had *exquisitely good taste*. Darcy chuckled and ducked into the hallway, having seen Elizabeth leave just a moment earlier.

"Are you on your way to see your father?" Darcy asked, bounding up the stairs two at a time and leaving Bingley and Richard to tend to the ladies in the drawing room without him. He had something more important to do than to play cards, and that something involved the lady who was slipping away from her sisters and was alone on the stairs.

Elizabeth halted her ascent and waited for him to join her. "I am. I only wished to see if he needed anything. We have been gone from him so much today. I cannot imagine how excessively tiring it must be to lie in one's bed and look at the same ceiling and walls for days."

"I would think it is rather boring." Darcy offered her his arm. "Are you planning to return to the drawing room after you have seen him."

Elizabeth sighed. "I am not certain I wish to hear my sisters argue over yet another thing." She smiled sheepishly. "You appear to be weathering their visit far better than I."

"I do not know them so well as you. If I did, perhaps I would find the end of my patience more quickly, but as it is, my store of vexation is rather empty compared with yours." The comment elicited a light, musical laugh of pleasure from Elizabeth. "I was hoping we could find a moment this evening to continue our discussion from earlier today."

"About shopping?"

Her question was said softly, but she did not turn away from his gaze as they stood at the top of the staircase. The welcome he saw in those lovely eyes buoyed his heart even further than her visit to his study had earlier today.

"I believe it was *more* than shopping we were to discuss." Much more. Infinitely more important than shopping. His future happiness was to be determined with this discussion.

She looked to her right and then her left. "There is no one in the hall. We could walk and talk, could we not?"

"We managed it at the Johnson's ball," he replied with a nod of his head toward his right before he started walking that direction with her on his arm.

"Indeed, we did – for a time."

He glanced at her. An impertinent smile graced her face just as the tone of her voice had indicated it did. He knew to what she was referring. At the Johnson's ball, they had only walked to the end of the hall, but that walk and the several minutes they spent standing at the far end of that hallway had been most pleasurable.

"This hall has an end just as the one at the ball," he replied with a smile of his own.

"Oh, so it does!"

Darcy chuckled. He did enjoy her teasing nature. It was so light and urged him to leave behind the heaviness of his more naturally austere temperament. She balanced him in that way, which was likely why he felt so steady in her presence. It was not that he was a wavering sort of fellow — he most certainly was not — but he did often feel awkward and ill-at-ease. But not here. Not with her. Not any longer.

"Did you see any shops we should visit?" he began.

She nodded. "I did. There are several that simply intrigue me too much never to explore them — not that I wish to purchase anything in them," she added hurriedly.

"You may if you wish," he replied. "That is if there are things within the shops that you would like."

"It is fortunate I am not my mother," she said with a laugh, "or a great number of things – necessary or not – would be added to your account."

He chuckled. "Your father mentioned that your mother likes to shop. Richard's mother is the same."

"And your mother? Did she like to shop?"

"She did. However, she was more cautious with her expenditures than my aunt is. In our family, it was my father who spent more lavishly than my mother."

"Then, you got your cautious nature from her?"

"A great part of it," he replied with a nod. "My father was so sure of himself. He was a bit like Richard in that regard, although I think Richard is more miserly. Not that my father was not a careful manager. He was wise in his decisions, most times."

There had been a few decisions made regarding Wickham which were perhaps more heart than head, but for the most part, his father had been sensible in his thinking.

"Then you have received your wisdom from him?"

Darcy shrugged. "Perhaps."

"Your sister is lovely," Elizabeth said softly. "Someone is responsible for that, and I do not think it is all your parents' doing."

He blew out a breath and looked toward the ceiling. "How do you know she is the reason I doubt my ability?"

It was so unusual to find anyone who understood him even when he explained himself. Bingley still struggled at times to comprehend how

Darcy thought about some things. Yet, Elizabeth seemed to have an innate ability to reason out things about his character that were often misunderstood. At least, she seemed to possess that skill tonight even if a few weeks ago her understanding had been clouded by his poor behaviour.

"Because I would feel the same," Elizabeth replied. "Even if it were not my fault that one of my sisters was placed in harm's way, I would feel as if I should have known, as if I should have seen the danger before it was present." She shrugged. "I imagine that is how many people feel about the ones they love."

He nodded and pulled her just a tiny bit closer to his side as they stood at the end of the hall, looking back in the direction they had come. "I love you – so very much," he said softly, "and I would feel even more doubtful of my abilities if I could not protect you from harm."

Elizabeth squeezed his arm and gave him a wavering smile when he looked down at her. "I would feel the same about you."

"You would?" His heart skipped a beat.

She nodded.

"Why?"

"I imagine," her smile turned slightly teasing, "that is how a lady feels about the gentleman she loves."

"You love me?" Oh, he knew he was smiling in a very stupidly broad fashion, but it could not be helped. The one thing for which he had longed for since November had come true. She loved him. And when something as wonderful as that occurs, one does not refrain from showing his pleasure.

"So very much," she replied.

He turned and took her hands in his. "Will you marry me?"

She nodded, her own smile growing with each bob of her head. "I will. Most happily."

He dropped her hands and wrapped his arms around her. "You have made me the happiest of men," he murmured as he held her to his heart.

Her arms wound their way around his waist. The sigh she expelled was a sound that matched the contentment which settled into his soul as he held her – his Elizabeth.

After a few moments, he released her but just barely, holding her in place with one arm.

"May I kiss you?" he asked as he cupped her cheek with his free hand.

Her cheeks glowed a lovely rosy colour as she formed the word "yes" with lips which he claimed before they had finished speaking.

Chapter 21

"Do you still wish to go see your father?" Darcy asked Elizabeth sometime later as she stood wrapped in his arms.

"I do." She did not want to leave where she was, but she also knew that the longer she stood here, the greater chance there was of someone discovering them and their wonderful news. And that news was something that she did not wish to share with anyone just yet. She wanted to keep this quiet, special moment to herself for just a while longer.

"May I accompany you?" He looked down at her. "He will be happy to know our news."

The smile that greeted her as she looked up at him was the sort that made her heart skip a beat. His face seemed to mirror her own feelings, for he looked completely, perfectly, thoroughly happy, and it was unspeakably wonderful to know that she was the cause of his joy just as he was of hers.

"Only him," she said softly. "I would like for this to be our secret for tonight if possible."

He chuckled. "I cannot promise that I will not give away something of it. Richard and Bingley will know, and I must tell them."

She understood that feeling as well. "And I must tell Jane and Papa, but if Mama and my other sisters could learn about it in the morning..."

"If your father is amenable," Darcy replied.

Then, sadly, he released her and, winding her arm around his, led her to her father's room.

"How do I look?" she whispered before he opened the door. Would her father be able to tell she had been kissing and embracing Mr. Darcy?

"You are blushing, but you look lovely." He shook his head as if he understood her thoughts. "Your father will suspect we have sealed our promise with a kiss, for that is how these things often happen. However, you do not look as if you were being improper." He lowered his voice just a touch further. "It is not improper to kiss your betrothed," he added.

That last comment did nothing to cool her

cheeks, but the thought of being able to kiss him again did cause her smile to grow. Oh, how she loved him. She squeezed his arm tightly, and he bent to kiss her lips quickly.

"Ready?" he asked as he turned the handle to open the door.

She nodded as she blew out a breath. Happy anxiousness fluttered in her belly.

"Ah, my Lizzy and Mr. Darcy," Mr. Bennet greeted. "I was hoping for a bit of distraction this evening, but knowing Mr. Bingley is here, I thought I might not be so fortunate."

"We could not leave you alone all evening," Mr. Darcy said as he pulled a chair close to where Elizabeth had taken a seat next to the bed. "Although I must admit it was Elizabeth's idea, I was happy to join her."

"Elizabeth is it?" Mr. Bennet asked with a chuckle.

"Yes," Darcy replied.

"Then you have happy news for me?"

"Only if you can keep a secret from Mama until tomorrow," Elizabeth said.

"I kept our trip to London a surprise until we

were nearly gone," he replied. "Are you betrothed?"

"Yes, if you will allow it," Elizabeth replied.

"I would not like to be the one to explain my refusal to your mother! She has taken as strong a liking to your Mr. Darcy as she held a disliking for him after the assembly."

Darcy shook his head. "A foolish, ill-thought-out comment, and utterly untrue."

"Yes, that would be how my wife would describe it," Mr. Bennet agreed with a chuckle. "However, she would not say it so concisely. I do believe she went on about it for a quarter hour upon her arrival home from the assembly and that was not the only time I heard it. But," he scooted up a bit in his bed and grimaced as he pulled his leg along, "that is the past. I am pleased to give you both my blessing. Though I do not like the thought of losing my Lizzy, I know that there is no better gentleman to whom I would see her tied."

"Thank you," Darcy mumbled.

Elizabeth smiled at his apparent embarrassment in being praised. "In this, my father, I do believe you are perfectly correct, for I can think of no gentleman better suited to me," she bit her lip and ducked her head, "or that I could love half as well as I do Mr. Darcy."

"It does my old heart good to hear it, my dear, for you know that your mother and I would do anything to see you girls happy and loved."

"I know," Elizabeth replied. "Now, how can we entertain you?"

"You have guests," her father cautioned.

"We will return to them in a few minutes," Darcy assured him. "For now, we would like to be of service to you."

"A game of chess then?" he asked.

Darcy willingly obliged and arranged the chessboard. "I have suffered defeat enough today. Perhaps Elizabeth would like a turn."

Mr. Bennet chuckled. "What say you, Elizabeth? Shall we play as we talk about weddings and such?" He held up a finger. "But no lace, I will not speak of lace."

Elizabeth laughed. "Mama did find a lovely piece of lace for me today."

"I know," her father said with a pointed look. "I heard all about the lace, the slippers, the gloves." He shook his head.

"And Mrs. Salter?" Elizabeth asked quietly.

His brows drew together. Apparently, her mother had not mentioned that part of their trip to her father.

"Who is Mrs. Salter?"

Elizabeth tipped her head. "Maybe I am not supposed to tell you."

"My curiosity is not going to be satisfied until you tell me more."

That was something Elizabeth had in common with her father. They were both curious creatures.

"Mama said that her name was Miss Foster before she married."

Her father's eyes grew wide. "Miss Foster, you say?"

Elizabeth nodded.

"Well, that could not have been pleasant. Miss Foster was always disagreeable." He shook his head. "Excessively disagreeable. Especially when she did not get what she wanted." He looked at Darcy. "Far worse than Miss Bingley. Miss Bingley appears to have some redeeming qualities should she be directed properly. Miss Foster was not so fortunate." He motioned for Elizabeth to begin playing.

"She was cunning." Again, he shook his head.

"What did Miss Foster have to say? And there is no need to tell me of her greeting and such. I just want to know how she attempted to disparage your mother."

Elizabeth sighed. "Will Mama be angry that I have told you?"

He shook his head. "She will tell me later." He smiled softly at Elizabeth. "After she has had time to put her shame and hurt away."

Unexpectedly, Elizabeth felt tears gather in her eyes which caused her to blink. Her father was so understanding of her mother. It was not something that was always displayed, but it did appear now and again. To hear him speak so softly now when her understanding of love for another was greater than it had ever been, she could hear that same love she felt for Mr. Darcy in her father's words.

"She has two sons and one daughter," Elizabeth began.

Her father sighed. "And your mother has five daughters."

It was stated as fact, but there was a small amount of pain in his voice as he spoke. Again, Elizabeth was struck by the love he held for her mother.

"She mentioned that and hoped that your estate was not entailed."

Mr. Bennet looked at Mr. Darcy. "The lady is from Hertfordshire and knows full well that Longbourn is entailed."

Darcy shook his head. "Some ladies can be vicious."

"Miss Foster – what did you say her name is now, Lizzy?"

"Mrs. Salter," Elizabeth replied.

"Mrs. Salter is among the champions of such ladies," he continued speaking to Darcy. "Did she say much else?" he asked, turning back to his daughter.

Elizabeth bit her lip.

Her father groaned. "She mentioned something about an indiscretion."

Elizabeth nodded. "And Mama had Jane tell Mrs. Salter her birthday."

Mr. Bennet shook his head. "That woman! Was that the extent of it?"

"No, she began to say that Jane's birthday was not proof that an indiscretion had not occurred, but she did not complete the full thought, though anyone listening would know what it was. Speculating in such a way, she said, was not what well-bred people did. Mary agreed with her and pointed out that well-bred ladies prefer to gossip in private."

Mr. Bennet chuckled.

"And then Mama told Mrs. Salter exactly how each of us is like you in some way and ended by saying if the lady could not appreciate those qualities, such as Mary's quick tongue, then she could never have truly admired you."

A smile spread across his face. "Ah, that is my Fanny," he said softly.

The room fell into silence for a few moments as father and daughter took turns playing.

"Your mother had gone to visit a friend in town. Someone she had met from school. All was well and good until the young woman's grandmother arrived unannounced." He darted a look at Darcy. "She was a lady of quality who did not approve of the smallest tie to trade."

Darcy grimaced. "I know some who are like that."

"She turned Fanny out." He blew out a breath. "Fanny cannot tell left from right when travelling. She wandered for hours with her bag in her hand.

It was fortunate that I had gone to this friend's home to call on Fanny, for upon hearing what had transpired, I was able to go in search of her." He sighed. "I found her and took her back to my apartment since it was very late, and Gardiner was not expecting her. He was not yet fully his own man in business, you see. It was perhaps a foolish thing for me to have done, but I needed to see her safe."

"And that was the indiscretion?" Elizabeth asked quietly.

He nodded. "There was no indiscretion aside from your mother being alone with me in my apartment, but Miss Foster heard of Fanny's expulsion into the streets and discovered the remaining details to which she added several of her own concoction. Fanny's father demanded that we marry within three weeks, for he could not imagine there had been no true indiscretion. His daughter was beautiful, and he himself was not above flirting with a pretty lady even though he was married." Her father's voice was harsh. "Just because a lady is the most beautiful woman you have ever beheld, does not mean..." His words trailed off as he shook his head.

"It is called self-control," Darcy said firmly, "and respect for the lady you love."

"Precisely!" Mr. Bennet said with some force. "I knew I liked you for a reason," he added with a chuckle.

"Check," Elizabeth said.

"Well, Mr. Darcy, it appears I can be beaten. You shall just have to ask me to share a somewhat troubling tale the next time we play." He laughed and forfeited his king. "Will you send your mother to me when you go below?"

"You will not tell her?" Elizabeth asked.

"Not a word, my dear, but I do need to remind her that she is the one my heart chose."

Again, Elizabeth blinked at sudden tears. Then, rising, she gave her father's cheek a kiss before following Darcy from the room.

Chapter 22

Later that evening, after Georgiana, Lydia, and Kitty had retired to Georgiana's room to play with Dash and discuss dresses and hats, and who knew what else, while Elizabeth and Jane had gone to visit their father once more before bed, Darcy sat in one of the corners of the drawing room with a snifter of brandy at his side and a book that he had no desire to read on his lap. Bingley had left some time ago, and Richard, who had seen the younger ladies and Dash to their room, was just returning to join Darcy.

"She said yes," Darcy said before Richard could even take his seat.

"You offered?"

Darcy nodded. "I did." A smile spread across his face as he considered his good fortune. "And she accepted. However, she does not wish for her mother to know until tomorrow. She wished to tell Miss Bennet first."

"Betrothed." There was a hint of awe in Richard's voice as he said the word. "I knew it would happen, but..." He shook his head. "Betrothed. Mother and Father will be pleased to know that there will finally be a Mrs. Darcy."

"I hope they are." Darcy knew that Elizabeth was not exactly the sort of lady whom Lady Matlock would have chosen for Darcy to court and marry. Elizabeth was nothing like the ladies to whom his aunt had introduced him. Though she lacked the standing in society which those ladies held, Elizabeth was far superior to any of them.

"They will be," Richard assured him. "Hopefully, Mother will then give up her notion that I need a wife." He tipped his glass and watched the contents sway with the action.

"You do eventually need a wife," Darcy replied. "I had almost begun to think you were considering the need now." He took a sip from his glass as Richard glanced at him. "You were talking about giving up your commission, and I thought perhaps there was more of a reason than just seeing Georgiana through her season."

Richard shook his head.

"No other reason?" Darcy pressed.

Again, Richard shook his head — more firmly this time. "I cannot consider such things until I am no longer married to my commission, and things are so uncertain..." his voice trailed off as if he were actually thinking about some lady and how such uncertainty would affect her.

"She is young."

Richard's head snapped up from his contemplation of the glass in his hand.

"Miss Lydia." Darcy waited for Richard to say something, but he did not, which spoke far more loudly than any protest would have about where Richard's thoughts and heart lay. "Would your mother approve?"

Richard placed his glass on a table and rose. "No. I do not think she would. She has aspirations for her children..." He ran a hand through his hair.

"She will be the sister of my wife."

Richard pulled in a deep breath as he nodded. "She is not at all what Mother would expect. She is not even the sort of lady I would have expected to capture my interest." He shook his head. "It is mere infatuation, nothing more. I will return to my unit. She will return to her home, and all will be as it should be."

Darcy raised a brow but said nothing.

"It will be," Richard repeated, "eventually."

It was Darcy's turn to shake his head. "I hope you are correct, for if you are not, the pain of separation I suffered after leaving Netherfield is not something I would wish on anyone, let alone you. You are my cousin and Georgiana's guardian. I would see you happy even if it were to cause a rift in our family. And, as my wife's sister, I would see that Mis Lydia was settled appropriately into a marriage. I know her father can only provide so much."

Richard shook his head. "I could not accept such charity."

Darcy smiled. "I know, that is why I will give it to her as a gift through her father."

Richard chuckled and rolled his eyes. "I had forgotten you have delved into your scheming nature, but we speak of things that will likely never be."

Darcy shrugged. He had attempted the same sort of arguments with himself before he left Netherfield, and he knew that Richard was no less stubborn than he himself was. Therefore, there was little use in debating the point with the man. He watched as his cousin took two more turns of the room before sitting down. "Not a word of this conversation leaves this room."

"Not a word."

"No matter how Bingley might taunt."

"Not a word," Darcy repeated.

"And no compromises."

Darcy laughed. "None. Unless one becomes necessary."

"She is lively and pretty," Richard muttered before slipping into silent contemplation of his glass once more. "Charming," he said breaking the silence. "She is charming."

"And in want of instruction?" Darcy asked.

Richard nodded. "There is that." He chuckled. "I shudder to think what she might say or do in the presence of my mother's friends. And that is yet another reason why this is not a good idea."

Again, Darcy was reminded of his own arguments against accepting his growing admiration for Elizabeth when he was in Hertfordshire. He had not feared her behaviour causing any raised brows, but he had feared the actions of her family would.

"I like them," he said aloud.

"You like whom?" Richard asked in surprise.

"The Bennets. I had thought I would not. I thought I would merely learn to tolerate them, but the more I know of them, the more I like them."

"Indeed? How so?"

"Mr. Bennet is indulgent, but he loves his family greatly. He knows his faults in that regard and admits them willingly. Only a man of true character would do so. And he is sharp. Such a keen mind!"

"But would not a man of character also take action to amend his ways."

Darcy had considered that very thing. "He may take action once his leg heals."

"And if not?"

That was a good question, and Darcy weighed it carefully. "Perhaps I could lend some aide? Just as you are with Miss Lydia?" He shook his head. "They have been exposed to a limited amount of good society here with you and Georgiana, and they have responded well to the setting. Granted it has only been a short time, and the setting is new, but if they were to experience society here in town..."

Richard nodded. "It could work. Mrs. Bingley and Mrs. Darcy could see that their sisters were given appropriate instruction and opportunity to be part of a finer society."

"They are not as horrid as I had first thought." Darcy's mouth tipped up on one side. "But then, I was not in any mood to be pleased when I was in Hertfordshire."

Richard chuckled as Darcy knew he would, for Richard had heard Darcy's grumblings about leaving home and spending an extended amount of time with Miss Bingley in the country – country where he knew no one but his host.

"That covers the father and the younger Bennets, but what of their mother?"

Darcy blew out a great breath. "She is not astute, but I believe her heart is good. Do you not remember how she responded to learning about Wickham?"

"That was impressive."

"She wishes to see her daughters avoid the trials she has endured."

Richard's brows drew together in question.

"I cannot say more than that. It would be wrong, but suffice it to say, Miss Bingley is not the only devious woman with whom Mrs. Bennet has been acquainted. In fact, Miss Bingley seems not so bad after hearing the tale Mr. Bennet shared with Elizabeth and me." He shook his head again. "She was a tradesman's daughter who became a gentleman's wife."

The comment was met with an understanding nod from Richard. They both knew how some could, and did, treat those whom they imagined to be their inferiors.

"Aunt Catherine will not be pleased," Richard said.

"Indeed, she will not be."

Their aunt was one who enjoyed feeling superior to all around her. She was the daughter of an earl and the wife of a baronet. Those two facts entitled her, in her mind, to a great deal of deference.

Richard drained the last of the liquid from his glass and rose. "You are getting married."

"I am." The joy that such a thing brought to Darcy's heart and mind was overwhelming. Elizabeth would be his Mrs. Darcy.

"Come along, old man." Richard motioned toward the door. "You and Mrs. Bennet have an exciting day ahead of you tomorrow. You'll need your sleep."

"I am not old," Darcy said as he rose to follow

Richard while he hoped, that in his happy state, he would be able to sleep.

"Married, old, are they not one and the same?" Richard teased.

"No," Darcy said as they entered the hall. "They are not the same."

Chapter 23

Elizabeth lay awake for some time after she and Jane had discussed, at length, their good fortunes in securing the affections of men such as Mr. Darcy and Mr. Bingley. Jane was now breathing softly and evenly next to her, but for Elizabeth, the excitement she felt when she thought of this room being just one of the guest rooms in her home would not allow her to relax enough to join her sister in sleep.

She sighed and closed her eyes.

Mrs. Darcy. It would be a wonderful name to wear, for with it came the love of Mr. Darcy. She pressed her fingers to her lips as she recalled his kisses and wrapped her arms around herself as she imagined being held in his embrace. Why had no one ever told her how lovely such things were? It was likely because once one knew...

Her thoughts trailed off as she heard something in the hall in front of her door.

She sat up in bed and listened.

Yes, there. That was a door, and if she was not mistaken, it was the one directly across the hall. Was her mother or one of her sisters unwell? She put on her slippers and robe before sneaking quietly into the corridor.

"Lydia," she called in a whisper to the disappearing form of her youngest sister. "Lydia," she called again as she hurried toward the staircase. "Where are you going?"

Lydia looked back at her sister and held a finger to her lip, indicating that Elizabeth should be quiet. However, there was no way Elizabeth was going to remain silent when her sister was sneaking around Darcy House in the middle of the night.

Elizabeth scampered down the stairs after Lydia. "Lydia!" she called in a louder whisper as Lydia moved toward the front door. Where was she going and at this hour?

"I will only be a minute," Lydia called back.

She turned into the sitting room, and Elizabeth sighed in relief. Lydia must have left something in there.

"Lydia, you frightened..." Elizabeth did not finish the sentence as she took in the aspect of an empty sitting room with an open window.

"Lydia?" Elizabeth called through the window before exiting the house herself in hopes of finding her sister — which she did. However, Lydia was not just outside the window; she was running down the street. Elizabeth chased after her, turning the corner just after her sister had, but stopped short the sight before her.

"Lydia!" Elizabeth's heart leapt to her throat as a gentleman extended his hand from a carriage, and Lydia climbed in.

"Are you coming, too?" Lydia asked, poking her head out of the still open door.

"I am not getting into a carriage in the middle of the night dressed as I am, and you are getting out."

"Oh, I will get out in just a moment. I only need to give my reply, and then we can return home," Lydia assured her. "But you do not want to stand on the street in the damp night air, do you?" She put her hand out to her sister.

"You must get out," Elizabeth demanded.

"I cannot. Not just yet," Lydia replied.

Elizabeth sighed and accepted Lydia's help into

the carriage. As foolish as she knew it was to enter that vehicle, there was no way she was going to let her sister sit in there with some gentleman unchaperoned. Why what if the man drove off with Lydia still in the carriage? She would never forgive herself for not having attempted to see to Lydia's safety.

"It is good to see you," the gentleman occupant of the carriage said as Elizabeth settled into her place next to Lydia.

"Mr. Wickham?" Her shock was so great at seeing him that had a cat batted at her as it did a length of yarn, it surely would have knocked her over.

"At your service," he pulled the door closed and tapped the roof of the vehicle.

"Where are we going?" Elizabeth demanded.

"Scotland," Wickham replied.

Elizabeth clutched the top of her robe at her throat. "Scotland?" she squeaked, her eyes darting from her sister to Wickham in the dim light from the exterior lanterns that filtered through the windows.

"No, we are not going to Scotland," Lydia replied. "That is what I have come to tell Wickham. We had intended to run away and marry. I thought it would be a great lark. However, I have changed my mind."

"What do you mean, you have changed your mind, my dear?"

Wickham's tone did not sound pleased to Elizabeth, and she sent a silent prayer heavenward that Providence would keep them safe.

"I do not love you."

"One does not need to be in love to marry," Wickham argued.

"But I should like to be, and while I do not love you, I think I might love another. And that would make being married very awkward, do you not agree?"

Elizabeth sucked in a breath. Lydia thought she was in love with Colonel Fitzwilliam?

"Has Darcy turned your head?" Wickham asked with a laugh. "He is rather old and dour for a pretty young thing such as you."

"Oh, no!" Lydia swatted Wickham's knee. "But he is not so terrible as you said. He has been very kind, although that might be because he is in love with my sister."

Wickham threw back his head and laughed

heartily. "I suspected as much when I met him in Hertfordshire."

"You did?" Elizabeth pressed her lips together. She should not have said anything.

"You are surprised to know that I knew of his admiration for you, but you have yet to protest that admiration."

"Only because she is as in love with him as he is with her," Lydia explained, much to Elizabeth's dismay.

"Indeed?" An unpleasant smile crept across Wickham's face.

"But Mr. Darcy is not half so gallant as his cousin," Lydia added dreamily.

Wickham's head whipped from his observation of Elizabeth toward Lydia. "Fitzwilliam?"

"Colonel Fitzwilliam," Lydia said with a sigh.

"He is even older and more unpleasant than Darcy," Wickham said.

"He is wonderful, and he is a colonel and the son of an earl."

"After his money, are you?"

Lydia shook her head. "No. He does not have all that much, but it should be adequate."

The carriage drove along silently for a time, making several turns, before Wickham tapped the top of the carriage signalling for it to stop.

"What are you doing?" Lydia asked as he opened the door.

"If you are not going to Scotland with me, then you should not be in this carriage."

"But we are not returned to Darcy House," Lydia protested. "I cannot just get out anywhere you choose."

"You can, and you will. Out!" He pointed toward the door. "I shall have you removed if you do not remove yourself."

Lydia gasped.

"Out!" he shouted inches away from her face.

"You are not nice," Lydia said with a flip of her head before poking Elizabeth in the side. "It seems we must walk home."

"I do hope you can find it," Wickham said with a sneer. "And I hope your colonel and his cousin will still accept you when it becomes known you were walking the streets late at night dressed as you are."

Elizabeth wrapped an arm around Lydia's shoulders.

"They will!" Lydia shouted at the carriage as the door closed. "They are gentlemen unlike you!"

She stamped her foot.

"Oh, of all the rotten things to do!"

"Shhh," Elizabeth said, trying to calm Lydia even as her own heart and mind raced. "We do not need to attract undue attention." She was not exactly certain how one got to Scotland, but this did not look like it was the correct direction. She looked up and down the unfamiliar street. There was a light in a window not far down the road, and people seemed to be moving about at the door. Perhaps she could inquire as to where they were and from that find her way back to Mayfair.

"Do not tell anyone where we are staying," she hissed in Lydia's ear. "And do not use your name." This did not appear to be an affluent neighbourhood, and she feared what some of the people here might do if they thought she and Lydia had any money of their own.

"Then who shall I say I am if someone asks?"

"You are Grace — it is one of your names — Grace ... Gardiner — after Mama, and I am your sister Ann." Elizabeth's mind whirled as she concocted their story. "We are staying in Gracechurch Street. If we can get there, we can get home." How she longed to be safe inside Darcy House at this moment! "Our carriage broke down three streets back," she whispered. "But I do not know how to explain the way we are dressed. Why did you have to go out at night, Lydia?"

Lydia pursed her lips and glared at Elizabeth. "I am Grace."

Though Lydia's expression was defiant and her chin lifted, Elizabeth could see the sheen of tears in her sister's eyes.

"I am sorry," Elizabeth replied. "I should not lecture at present."

"I did not think he would toss us out on the street."

Elizabeth could hear the trembling in her sister's voice. Those tears were likely to start falling at any moment.

"That is understandable." She rubbed her sister's arm soothingly while her own heart hammered in her chest. "All will be well," she murmured as comfortingly as she could. "All will be well." She only hoped her words were true.

Chapter 24

Elizabeth and Lydia trudged a distance down the road before Lydia asked quietly, "Why would he do such a thing?"

Elizabeth could hear the hurt in Lydia's voice and responded gently, "Because, he is not what he appears. The stories he told about Mr. Darcy are lies, and, well..." She paused and pulled her sister closer as she considered how Darcy's sister Georgiana had been duped by Wickham. "I must know something, Lydia."

Her sister nodded.

"Was it your plan to elope or his?"

There was a long moment of silence during which Elizabeth thought perhaps her sister would not answer. However, she did.

"I am not entirely certain."

"What do you mean?"

"I joked with him and his friends once about how I would likely be the first of all five of us sisters to marry. I was only flirting. But then, one day sometime later, Wickham suggested that I could ensure that I was the first to marry if I were to marry him."

"Did he make you an offer of marriage?"

Lydia shook her head. "Not in so many words. It was more of a suggestion and not a request."

"When did this happen?"

"Oh, it was when I was telling him all about the ball at Netherfield. He was very sorry to have missed it and the chance to dance with both you and me and doubly sorry that you had been forced to dance with both Mr. Collins and Mr. Darcy. He laughed for some time about that actually." Her head ducked. "I did, too. It was not nice of me."

"I felt sorry for myself for having had to dance with them both," Elizabeth replied with a smile. "I had no idea just how wonderful Mr. Darcy was at that time."

"Nor did I," Lydia said with a small smile. "He is quite nice, is he not?"

Elizabeth squeezed her sister close and agreed

before urging her to continue telling her about Wickham.

"Wickham was surprised at Mr. Darcy dancing with you at first. 'What?' he said, 'Old, high and mighty Fitzwilliam Darcy condescended to dance with someone not in his circle? That is rich,' and then he dissolved into peals of laughter. Then he said, 'Do you know what would be an even better joke than Darcy dancing?' Of course, I did not, and that is when he said we should run away and marry because that would truly be something about which to laugh."

"Marriage is not something about which one should jest." Elizabeth kept her voice soft but firm.

Lydia sighed and rubbed the corner of one eye. "I know that now."

"Do you?" Elizabeth demanded.

Lydia nodded as she wiped her eyes with the sleeve of her robe. "I did not know one could feel anything more than a thrill of being admired until I came to Darcy House."

"Are you saying you love the colonel?"

Lydia's shoulders lifted and lowered. "I think I love him. He... he cares for me." A small silly grin tipped the corners of her mouth. It was an expression Elizabeth recognized, for she often wore it when thinking of Mr. Darcy. Her youngest sister was well and truly besotted.

"And I wish to please him." Lydia shook her head, her smile fading. "And I do not just wish for his admiration of my hair or clothes or anything. I want him to think well of me." She brushed tears from her cheek and once again lifted and lowered her shoulders sadly. "He will not after this."

Elizabeth pulled her sister close. "That is not what you told Mr. Wickham."

"I say lots of things to Wickham that are not true."

They had reached the house with the light in the window, so though Elizabeth wished to know what sorts of lies Lydia told Mr. Wickham and why Lydia seemed to think it acceptable to do so, they could not continue their conversation.

"Pardon me," she said as she stepped around a man who had just exited the house.

"What have we here?" he asked. "You must be new."

His words slurred, and Elizabeth could smell some sort of alcohol on his breath when he leaned close to look at her. He was not old or dirty as she had expected someone from this part of town to be. In fact, the hat and coat he nearly wore – his hat was askew, and his coat was only on one arm while the other arm of the garment dangled behind him – were of an excellent quality as was the cravat which hung undone around his neck.

"Sally!" He called back toward the house. "Your new girls are here."

Elizabeth's eyes grew wide, and she swallowed as she shook her head. "We are not Sally's girls." She was not exactly certain who Sally's girls were, but she had her suspicions and knew that she did not want to be thought of as such.

"Aye, they are a pair of pretty doxies!" the man shouted toward the door.

"Might we just pass?" Elizabeth attempted once again to step around him. "Our carriage wheel broke, and we need to know where we are."

"You are at Sally's," the man said with a sweep of his hand toward the house that nearly toppled him.

"Might we just pass?" Elizabeth asked once again.

"Aye, but not without a kiss."

"I think not!" Elizabeth replied firmly, causing

him to laugh and place a hand on her shoulder to keep from falling.

"How 'bout you?" His hand remained on Elizabeth's shoulder as he leaned toward Lydia.

"A shilling for one cheek and a half crown for both."

Both Lydia's reply and her boldness surprised Elizabeth.

"A shilling for a peck on the cheek?" the man exclaimed.

"Or a half crown for two," Lydia repeated.

"And if I do not wish for you to kiss my cheeks?"

"Then you must do without." Lydia batted her lashes and smiled as Elizabeth had seen her do on several occasions when Jacob Lucas was attempting to scheme his way out of doing something for Lydia and his sister, Maria. Elizabeth had to admit that when it came to getting what she wanted, Lydia was a proficient.

Lydia held out her hand. "A shilling for one, a half crown for two, or move aside so we might pass."

The man grumbled, dug around in the pocket of his coat once he had caught the flapping garment, and pushed a shilling in Lydia's hand.

Lydia wrapped her hand around the coin. "Which cheek?"

He turned his head to the right, exposing his left cheek.

Lydia pinched his nose which caused him to shout.

"I must guarantee you are not going to attempt to steal more than that for which you have paid," she said before giving his cheek a peck and then releasing his nose.

As he was busy rubbing his nose, Lydia pushed Elizabeth to move around him.

"A shilling for a kiss?" Elizabeth whispered. "Proper young ladies do not charge for kisses, and they do not kiss strangers – or friends." She knocked on the door.

"We are rid of him, are we not?" Lydia demanded. "And we now have one shilling which is far more than what we had a moment ago," she added as she stepped into the house behind Elizabeth.

"Who might you be?" A fashionably dressed woman leaned on an ornately carved cane and gave them both an appraising look.

"I am Ann, and this is my sister Grace."

The woman nodded and waited.

"Gardiner," Elizabeth added. "Ann and Grace Gardiner."

The woman's mouth dropped open and then snapped closed. "Gardiner, you say?" Her eyes narrowed, and she took a step nearer Lydia. "I knew a Gardiner once," she murmured as she scrutinized Lydia. "She looked a lot like you. Her name was Fanny."

"Mama?" The word leaped from Lydia's lip.

"If your mama is Fanny Gardiner who has a brother named Edward who works somewhere in town – near Cheapside, if I recall correctly," the woman replied.

"Oh, it is her!" Lydia cried. "Uncle Gardiner lives in Gracechurch Street, and his name is Edward."

"Hmm," the lady said with a chuckle, "Fanny Gardiner's girls." She shook her head. "Gardiner," she repeated tipping her head. "You say your family name is Gardiner? I had thought she would marry that handsome young man who came in here all afluster to get her. Bennet was his name."

"Papa?" Lydia's eyes were wide.

The lady chuckled. "Gardiner, is it?" she asked

Elizabeth. "Or is it Bennet?" She shook her head. "You do not need to tell me. I understand it might be best if your true names are not known in an establishment such as mine." She waved to a door on the right. "Come. You can sit in my apartment and tell me your tale of woe over a cup of moderately good tea."

She led the way, and Lydia and Elizabeth had no choice but to follow or be left in the entry way where that gentleman from outside might find them again.

"I am very good – excessively good – at keeping secrets," she said with a pointed look for them both before she allowed them to enter her private domain.

Chapter 25

"Fitzwilliam?"

Darcy rubbed his eyes and squinted through the darkness toward the door to his room. Had he heard his name amid the knocking?

"Fitzwilliam?"

There it was again.

"Please, open the door."

Hurriedly, Darcy donned his robe and padded over to open the door for his sister.

"Are you..." His question about her wellbeing died on his lips as he took in the aspect of tear stained cheeks on the young woman beside her. "Miss Kitty, what is wrong?"

"Lydia is gone. She was supposed to return an hour ago, but she has not?" These words were followed by sobs as Kitty buried her face in her hands.

Darcy nodded toward the chairs near his fire

which was burning low and, leaving the door fully open, crossed to his night stand to light another candle. The one which Georgiana carried was little more than a nub and did not give enough light for his liking.

"Has she told you what this is about?" He asked his sister as he returned to them and placed his candle on the table next to Georgiana's.

Georgiana lifted her chin in a very determined fashion and nodded. Darcy had seen her make that same expression before – usually when she was attempting not to cry. Something was seriously wrong.

"Miss Lydia went to meet someone."

"At night?" Darcy asked in surprise.

Georgiana nodded and swallowed. "Wickham," she whispered, tears glistening in her eyes.

"Wickham?" The question was expelled on a rush of air. Darcy gripped the arm of Georgiana's chair and knelt next to her. He sucked in a breath to replace the one which had been knocked out of him by his sister's revelation.

Georgiana nodded. "Miss Kitty came to me when Miss Lydia did not return, and I suggested we come to you."

"You have not informed Mrs. Bennet or any of Miss Lydia's sisters?"

"No, Mama would be so distressed," Kitty managed to say as she fought to keep from sobbing once again.

"What about Miss Bennet or Elizabeth?" Surely someone in the Bennet family must be told that Lydia was missing.

"I thought of that, but what can they do?" Georgiana asked. "Mr. Bennet cannot go searching for Miss Lydia, nor can any of her sisters. At least, they cannot go unaccompanied."

"Mr. Darcy," Mr. Abram stood at Darcy's door.

"Yes."

The butler took one step into the room. His brow furrowed slightly as he took in the sight of the Georgiana and Kitty. "I have the unpleasant task of informing you, sir, that a window has been left open in the drawing room. We have conducted a thorough search of the lower levels and not a thing appears to be out of place."

Darcy sighed. "Miss Lydia is out of place. Please have my horse readied and send up my man as soon as is possible."

"Miss Lydia?" Abrams repeated. No amount of

training could keep all the surprise and concern out of the Darcys' faithful servant's tone. "Shall I call for a horse for the colonel as well?"

Darcy nodded. "It would be best if I did not search alone." Richard had experience running wayward recruits aground, his assistance would be invaluable.

"Mr. Abrams," he called before his butler had done more than turn to leave.

"Yes, sir."

"Please, rouse the colonel and send him to me."

"Right away, sir."

Darcy turned back to his sister and Kitty and pushed the furry mass that rubbed against him away. "Not now Dash."

Dash poked him with his nose, then sniffed his way over first to Kitty and then to Georgiana before racing from the room.

"Did Miss Lydia tell you what she was going to do?" Darcy asked gently.

"She was supposed to meet Mr. Wickham and tell him that she did not wish to marry him."

"They were going to Scotland," Georgiana added in a whisper.

Darcy clutched her hand firmly. How difficult

this must be for her having to remember her own folly and plan to run away with the cad.

"I am well," she whispered. "Truly. But Miss Lydia is in danger."

Kitty dissolved into tears once again at the statement.

"I told her some of what passed at Ramsgate when she came to me. By doing so, I assured her that you would know what to do and would not treat Lydia poorly for her foolishness."

"I will never say a word," Kitty said through her tears. "Just please find my sister."

"What do you need?" Richard rubbed his face as he entered Darcy's room. "Is someone unwell?" he asked when he saw who was with Darcy.

"Lydia is gone," Kitty wailed.

Richard stopped dead halfway between the door and the hearth. "What do you mean 'gone'?"

Dash raced into the room, a piece of paper hanging from his mouth. He sat down in front of Richard and dropped the paper.

"She went to meet someone," Darcy said as his cousin bent to pick up what Dash had delivered to him.

Richard blanched as he unfolded the paper. "Wickham?" he nearly shouted.

Kitty burst forth with fresh sobs while Darcy nodded and Georgiana attempted to comfort her friend.

"Scotland? They are going to Scotland?" Richard demanded.

"No," Darcy said, rising from next to his sister. Kitty would be well cared for by Georgiana, and, at the moment, his cousin looked as if he was in greater need of attention. "She went to tell him that she did not wish to marry him."

"She went to tell him that he was not getting what he wanted?" Richard sneered. "That never ends well with someone like Wickham."

"Have a care," Darcy scolded. "Miss Kitty is distressed enough. She does not need you to add to her worry." He grabbed Richard by the arm and pulled him into the hall. "I have sent for our horses, and as soon as we are dressed, we will begin a search."

"Where?" Richard demanded. "We do not know which road he took or if he tricked her into..." His jaw clenched, and he did not continue.

"I was hoping you might know where we could

find him in town. If we find where he was staying, then perhaps we can find out where he has gone or if he returned disappointed."

"He'll pay, and you'll not stop me," Richard's voice was low and dangerous.

"I will not see you hang," Darcy cautioned.

"I shall do my best to leave him living."

"Mr. Darcy," Jane said as she approached him. "Have you seen Elizabeth? Did she pass this way? She is not with our father."

Darcy's heart plummeted to his stomach.

"Do you still wish for him to live?" Richard asked quietly.

Darcy shook his head. "I wish for you to live," he replied.

"Do you know where Elizabeth is?" Jane asked.

Again, Darcy shook his head. "We will search the house, but..." He turned back toward his room. "Is it possible she might have heard Lydia and followed her?"

"What do you mean?"

Darcy had never heard quite so much emotion in Miss Bennet's voice.

"Miss Kitty has informed us that your youngest

sister left some time ago to meet Wickham and tell him she did not wish to marry him."

Richard caught Jane by the elbow and, wrapping an arm around her, held her upright. "We were just going to prepare to find Miss Lydia."

"Georgiana," Darcy called, "please take Miss Bennet and Miss Kitty to your sitting room." He turned to Jane. "I will inform your father of what is afoot before I leave. However, I will need to leave your mother to you. Are you able to care for her?"

Jane nodded.

"Allow me to assist you to Georgie's room," Richard offered.

"What is happening?" Mrs. Bennet stuck her head out of her door.

"Come with me, Mama," Jane said. "There is something I must tell you."

A wave of compassion swept over Darcy as he saw the concern in Mrs. Bennet's eyes.

"Is everyone well?" she asked, clutching her robe at the neck. "Kitty, why are you in Mr. Darcy's room?"

"Come, Mama," Jane repeated. "I will tell you, but not here."

Darcy placed a hand on Jane's arm. "I will return

her daughters to her, and I will do my best to see they are unharmed."

Jane pressed trembling lips together and nodded her head. "I know you will," she whispered, "and I will tell her so."

Chapter 26

Darcy and Richard saw that Jane, Kitty, Georgiana, and Mrs. Bennet were settled in Georgiana's sitting room before they began their preparations. Darcy began his with a brief, though difficult, visit to Mr. Bennet's room while Richard, followed by Dash, returned to his own room.

Richard was, of course, ready to leave before Darcy, and Darcy found him where he knew he would, pacing the front hall, while Dash raced up and down the stairs, along the corridor, and finally into the sitting room where he sat and barked at the window.

"See that he gets to Georgiana's room," Darcy said to Abrams as he joined Richard.

Richard shoved the note Dash had delivered to him at Darcy. "Look at the direction? That is not Wickham's hand. That looks feminine."

Darcy took note of the swooshes and swirls of the writing on the outside of the missive. It did indeed seem to have a feminine quality to it.

"It did not seem out of place," Abrams shuffled from one foot to the other nervously. "If I had known..."

"How could you?" Richard said. "For once, that idiot was clever." He shook his head.

Clever was seldom a word anyone used in conjunction with Wickham's name. However, this time, Darcy had to agree with Richard. This did appear to be a clever ploy. "When did it arrive?"

"This morning, sir."

Dash raced between them and up the stairs, a footman following close behind.

Darcy shook his head. That pup was a ball of energy even in the dead of night.

"Some tea or something slightly stronger might be needed by those above stairs." He put his hat on as he instructed Abrams.

"Of course, sir. We will see that they are well tended."

Darcy rested a hand on his butler's shoulder and nodded. It was a small sign of approval, but one that Abrams understood well. The staff at Darcy

House were exceptional at their jobs, and Abrams was one of the reasons for that. The man knew how to lead without being overbearing. The Bennets and his sister would be in good hands while he and Richard were gone, and Darcy wished for his butler to know he knew that. The small smile and nod Darcy received in return let him know his message had been understood.

Richard stood impatiently holding the door open as he waited for Darcy. However, it was Dash who reached the door before Darcy did, planting himself in front of Richard and growling viciously at the footman when he reached for him.

Richard scowled down at the dog, but his reprimand died on his lips when he saw something dangling from Dash's mouth. "What do you have there, boy?" He stooped and took a red ribbon from Dash.

Dash did not remain where he was to reply or to allow Richard to even rise. Instead, as soon as the ribbon was in Richard's hand, Dash ran to the horses, standing at the head of Richard's horse and looking for all the world as if he were demanding the beast's full attention and obedience.

"I think he wishes to help," Richard said with a

chuckle as Dash took his eyes off the horse to once again growl at the approaching footman before barking and running forward and then returning to stare down Richard's mount once again.

"Leave him be," Darcy said to the footman. "He will join us on our search."

Richard had swung up into his saddle. "Dash, up," he commanded, patting the front of his coat.

Dash trotted over, looked at the footman expectantly, and allowed the man to lift him up without so much as a whimper, let alone a growl.

"He's very much like Miss Lydia," Richard said as he scratched the dog's ear once he was settled in front of him. "Determined to have his way and compliant once he gets it."

Darcy sighed. "And causing trouble without meaning to do so."

Richard nodded, and the two gentlemen began riding. "We never gave her reason to doubt Wickham was anything more than what he presented."

"We had no reason to tell her anything," Darcy replied. "Where to?" He was confident that Richard had a plan in mind. His cousin would not be so calm as he was now if he did not already know where they were going to begin their search.

"Mrs. Younge's boarding house. If anyone knows where he is, she does. I would bet you a month's wages that she is the one who addressed that letter, but I am not the gambling sort. I do not like to be parted from my money."

Darcy chuckled, and then the two men fell into silence as they road. Darcy knew that if Richard's thoughts were anything like his own, that month's salary, as well as all Richard had, would be given away without a second thought to have both Lydia and Elizabeth back at Darcy House, safe in bed.

Thoughts of Elizabeth being found unharmed as well as thoughts of seeing Wickham laid out on the floor filled Darcy's mind as he rode.

"Ahead on the left," Richard said.

Dash, who had been lying down, sat up, alert to whatever was coming.

"Good boy." Richard scratched the dog's ear. "Bite his leg, and I'll give you a tin full of biscuits."

Dash yipped his understanding as Richard dismounted and reached up to lift him down.

Darcy was already at the door, banging loudly.

"What's the meaning of this noise?" A man shouted from behind the door.

"Open the door," Darcy yelled in response.

"Why should I?"

Richard pushed Darcy to the side and threw his shoulder against the door. "We need to see Mrs. Younge about a scoundrel," he called.

"No need to break the door," the man called back. Locks rattled, and finally, the door opened. "My mistress is abed as are all her guests."

Richard forced his way inside the door, Dash scooting between him and the man who had opened the door. "Is there a guest named Wickham?"

"Yes, sir." The candle the man held trembled slightly as Richard towered over him. "At the top of the stairs."

"He is here?" Darcy asked.

The man nodded. "Only just. Was gone for some time, but he tends to come and go at odd hours."

"Is he alone?" Richard demanded as he moved to the stairs.

"Tonight, he is, and he seemed none too pleased to be so. Took a bottle of port with him to his room." The man placed his candle on the table near the door and fished out a ring of keys from the pocket of his robe, fiddling with them until he had one between his fingers. "My mistress won't want no broken doors." He handed the key to Darcy. "Is it about a sister or a wife? You wouldn't be the first to seek him for such."

"Both," Darcy replied before hurrying up the stairs after Richard. "Wait!" he whispered loudly, holding up the key.

Richard gave a nod of his head and stood aside but only long enough for Darcy to open the door. Then, he entered the room before Darcy but after Dash, who leapt onto the bed with a bark and a growl.

"What the devil?" Wickham cried as he sat up in bed. "Who let this beast into my room?"

"I did," Richard said, leaning close to Wickham.

"What? Who?"

Darcy struck a match and lit a candle.

Wickham's eyes grew wide. "Fitzwilliam?" They shifted to Darcy. "Darcy?"

"You're not in Scotland," Darcy said.

Wickham smirked. "No need. I got what I wanted."

The crack of knuckles against jaw was the reply that greeted his lie.

Wickham scrambled from his bed, placing the

piece of furniture between him and Richard as he held his jaw. "She's sweet on you." He wiped blood from his lip with the back of his hand. "And you," he jutted his chin toward Darcy, "it seems, have actually managed to convince a lady to have you."

Darcy nodded. "Despite your lies."

"Where are they?" Richard shouted.

Dash leaned forward from the edge of the bed toward Wickham and growled to punctuate Richard's words.

"I have no idea."

Richard rounded the bed and grabbed Wickham by his nightshirt. "What do you mean you have no idea? Did they not meet with you? Were you not going to Scotland?"

Wickham laughed. "They met with me, but I had no intention of ever going to Scotland." His eyes narrowed as he looked around Richard to Darcy, who was at Richard's shoulder. "Never have had any plans to go to Scotland."

Darcy growled. Richard released Wickham and stood to the side, arms folded as Darcy expelled his displeasure on Wickham's person.

"Where are Elizabeth and her sister?" Darcy

asked as he stood over Wickham. His fist throbbed, but it was a satisfying pain.

"I have no idea. I opened the door, and they got out of the carriage." He scooted back toward the wall. "Somewhere between here and the river. Closer to the river."

Richard crouched down. "You best pray we find them within the hour, or we will return." He rose. "We may come back anyway."

Darcy smirked. "Perhaps he should go to Scotland," he said to Richard.

"That might be a good idea," Richard replied, "although I would still hunt him down there if anything – and I do mean anything — untoward has happened to either of them. Dash. Come."

Dash looked at Richard, then lurched at Wickham and growled before following Richard and Darcy from the room.

"Thank you," Darcy said, handing the keys back to the man at the bottom of the stairs. "We may return if we do not find what we are seeking."

The man's head bobbed up and down rapidly. "I'll open on the first knock," he assured them as they left.

Darcy blew out a breath as he stood on the

street, looking toward the river. "Between here and the river?"

Richard nodded. "Closer to the river."

"Wandering the streets," Darcy muttered. And frightened, but hopefully unharmed.

Richard wrapped the red ribbon from his pocket around his fingers and knelt next to Dash. "I don't know how good you are at hunting," he said, holding the ribbon out for Dash to sniff, "but I would sure appreciate some help finding Miss Lydia."

Chapter 27

Elizabeth pulled Lydia toward a rose-coloured sofa in Sally's comfortable sitting room. A book lay open on a table next to a chair near the hearth. Its presence surprised Elizabeth. How did one relax with a book of poetry while drunken men entered and exited one's establishment? She smoothed her robe and made certain that it was done up as well as it could be as she took a seat.

Though the place where she found herself made her feel excessively uncomfortable, Elizabeth would not deny that the warmth radiating from the fire felt wonderful as it wrapped around her, chasing away the coldness of the night and restoring feeling to her nose and toes.

"My name is not actually Sally. Just like you, I have no desire for my guests to know my real name, for various reasons." With a dismissive wave of her hand at her final words, she took her seat. The discussion of identities, as well as Sally's ability to keep a secret, appeared to be at an end. "The tea will be here soon along with some clothes. I think we have a girl or two who are about your size."

"Clothes?" Lydia asked in surprise. "We do not need clothes."

Sally chuckled. "You cannot be delivered to your uncle's home in the middle of the night dressed as you are." She sighed. "I would just allow you to sleep here, but it would not do for you to be seen exiting my establishment in the morning. A young gentleman can afford such whispers but not young ladies. Therefore, the cover of darkness will be to our advantage. We will have tea and then one of my footmen will accompany you to your uncle's home."

The woman tipped her head and looked at Lydia. "You are the very image of your mother."

"You remember her?" Elizabeth asked.

Sally nodded. "I know it would seem nearly impossible for one to remember a lady twenty-some years after meeting her, especially since our meeting was not long in duration, and, well, I do meet a good number of young women." She rose as a tray with three cups of tea arrived, carried by a young maid in a perfectly modest and rather drab dress.

"Your mother," Sally continued as she passed a cup of tea to Lydia and then Elizabeth, "was in quite a state when I found her."

"You found her? Where did you find her?" Lydia asked over the rim of her cup.

Sally chuckled. "Very like your mother. So inquisitive," she muttered before continuing. "She was walking up and down the street. I saw her pass the window there." She pointed to the window that would face the street. "She passed three times before I rose and watched her turn a corner and disappear only to reappear in front of my window not half an hour later." She took a sip of her tea. "She was walking in circles." This comment was followed by another chuckle and a shake of Sally's head before she took a sip of tea.

"I brought her in here, fed her, and dried her tears. Oh, the tears! But it was understandable."

"Why was she crying?" Lydia had moved to the edge of the sofa and was resting her elbows on her knees and her chin on her hands. Her cup of tea had been abandoned to a side table as she had become absorbed in the story.

Lydia had always been easily entertained by a story when just a girl, which was likely why she found gossip so delightful now that she was older.

"She had been turned out of her friend's house because she was not a gentleman's daughter," Elizabeth supplied.

"You know the story then?" Sally asked.

"As much as Papa told me just the other day."

"Papa told you? When?" Lydia asked.

"Do you remember Mama meeting Mrs. Salter when we were shopping?" Elizabeth asked.

Lydia's brow furrowed. "I think I do."

"You were helping Miss – our friend," Elizabeth corrected, "make a selection at the counter."

Lydia nodded.

"Papa told me on that day when I told him how upset Mama was by the things Mrs. Salter said."

"What did she say?" Lydia demanded.

"She hinted that Mama and Papa only married because of Jane." She held Lydia's gaze until she saw the widening of Lydia's eyes as understanding dawned.

"Oh, no!" Lydia shook her head adamantly. "Not Mama. Or Papa!"

"Your mother was no lightskirt," Sally inserted. "She gave a couple of gentlemen a good tongue lashing when they attempted to sit too close or touch her when she was here. No one was allowed such liberties unless he had a marriage certificate in his hand and a fortune in the bank. That's what she said. That and that even with all the gold in England, they would have to be a great deal more handsome, noble, and kind than Mr. Bennet if they wished to succeed with her, and she knew, just knew, that such a thing was not possible." Sally chuckled again. "She was a delight, and I am pleased to meet her daughters. No matter what their names may or may not be." She winked.

"We have three sisters," Elizabeth said. "No brothers."

"Indeed? I take it that your mama and that handsome man who came to collect her married?"

Elizabeth nodded.

"Do not worry. I have never in all my years mentioned your mother's name until I saw you, and you said your name was Gardiner." She shrugged. "I wouldn't have brought you in here if I did not know she was your mother. My girls never enter this room. It is my sanctuary. A step away from the work I do." She shrugged again. "A lady without a gentleman or her own fortune must find her way somehow, and I dislike both cleaning and cooking. Service was not for me." She leaned back with her teacup cradled in her hands. "I know it is not a proper occupation and my reasons for its existence will not meet with the approval of fine young women such as yourselves, but this has been my life. I live well, and I see that my girls are safe – or as safe as can be."

Elizabeth nodded and sipped her tea. She really did not wish to know what Sally did for a living or how well she ran her establishment.

"Ah, gowns," Sally said, sitting forward as the maid once again entered. "Place them on my bed," she instructed.

"Do you ladies have handsome young men who might come bursting through my door ready to cut down anyone who might attempt to stand in their path?" Sally continued.

"Lizzy does." Lydia's eyes grew wide, and she clamped her lips closed.

"I am good at keeping secrets," Sally reassured her before turning expectantly to Elizabeth.

"I am betrothed."

"You are what?" Lydia nearly shouted.

"I was going to tell Mama in the morning," Elizabeth explained. "I wished to keep it a secret until then." She shrugged and smiled sheepishly at Lydia. "I just wished to enjoy the wonderfulness of being his for a night without anyone else, save Papa and Jane, knowing."

"No one else knows?" Lydia bounced in her seat.

"Perhaps his cousin," Elizabeth replied.

"Colonel Fitzwilliam?"

"Fitzwilliam?" Sally repeated. "My, my, Fanny Gardiner's daughters have some high connections."

Lydia's hand covered her mouth.

Sally chuckled. "I swear I will not say a word." She tipped her head. "A cousin?" She waggled her brows at Elizabeth. "I think I know of whom you speak, though I would never expect to see him darken my door. He's not the sort, or so I have heard." She placed her empty cup on the table next to her book.

"Now," she said rising, "we should see you into

some more appropriate clothes for travel. We would not want your names bandied about as belonging to this establishment."

"There was a man out front who thought we were," Lydia said as she followed Sally.

It seemed Lydia had already accepted this woman they had just met as a friend. Lydia was like that. Elizabeth welcomed newcomers, but she held them at a distance until she could figure out their character. She shook her head – except when it was a handsome cad in a uniform telling her horrid tales about a gentleman she wished to hate.

"You said my Papa came here to get my Mama?"

Elizabeth chuckled. Of course, Lydia would wish to hear the rest of the tale.

Sally clasped the lovely green day dress she held to her chest. "Your mama saw your papa pass by the window and tripped over a footstool on her way to call to him through the window. I have never seen a lady so delighted to see a gentleman as she was." She passed the dress to Lydia. "And he was so gallant." She shook her head and sighed. "It is the kind of love story about which every young girl dreams – her prince coming to her rescue when she is in distress."

244

Lydia sighed. "Mama was very beautiful."

"Is," Elizabeth corrected. "Mama is very beautiful."

"Yes, but now she is married, and her beauty is not so important," Lydia replied.

Sally laughed. "You are the image of your mother. You may slip into this behind the screen. You can keep your nightgown on under it since you do not have a proper shift, but we will fold your robe and tie it up like a package. It's better to travel with a package and be a bit chilled than to wear the robe and have your reputation tarnished."

Chapter 28

"Do we go up this one?" Darcy nodded toward Fish Street Hill. One street was beginning to blend into another as the men searched for Lydia and Elizabeth. A fear that they had already been found by someone unsavoury had settled into Darcy's heart.

Richard blew out a breath and shook his head. "I don't know. Do you see anyone on the street?" He scratched Dash's head.

Apparently, his cousin was also beginning to feel the hopelessness Darcy was attempting to keep at bay. He had to find Elizabeth. He could not lose her. He looked up the street, sitting still and listening while he watched for any sign of movement.

"No," Darcy answered after a moment of watching. "Then we stick to Thames?"

Dash's bark made it impossible to hear Richard's reply, and the creature's popping to attention took a quick hand from the colonel to keep the beast from falling from his perch on Richard's horse.

"What is it, boy?" Richard asked as he attempted to quiet Dash. "That carriage?" He nudged his horse forward. A carriage was moving down the road in front of them.

"It is worth a look," Darcy said as he drew up next to Richard. "I do not think they would have money for the fare, but at this moment, I am willing to look anywhere."

"As am I," Richard replied. "It's stopping at Sally's."

Darcy tipped his head. "Sally's?"

Richard shrugged. "One of the places my brother helps finance with his allowance."

"A brothel?" Darcy knew that the viscount was given to some vices, and Sally's did not appear to be a gambling hall or tavern.

Richard nodded. "The only one he visits."

One was more than any gentleman should visit in Darcy's opinion.

"It is likely just some drunken chap finding his way – No, those are not gentlemen." Richard urged his horse to go faster as Dash once again took to barking.

In the light of the lamp outside the house just two blocks away, Darcy could make out the forms of two ladies in front of Sally's house and being handed into the hackney by a footman while another lady stood at the door giving instructions.

"Lydia?" Richard shouted. "Elizabeth?"

The lady in the doorway waved and the ladies who had just boarded the carriage were removed from it.

It was them. It had to be them. Darcy expelled a breath as relief washed over him at the thought. His Elizabeth was safe. He did not reach the house before Richard, but Dash had only just been handed to Lydia who was exclaiming about being rescued just like her mother when Darcy arrived.

Darcy dismounted and dropping the reins of his horse, rushed to Elizabeth, enveloping her in his embrace. "I found you," he whispered to her hair, "I was afraid I would not."

Elizabeth held on to him tightly.

He pulled back just a little so that he could look at her face. "You are well? You have not been injured?"

"Thanks to Sally, we are well," Elizabeth replied,

smiling brightly at him even though her eyes glistened with unshed tears.

Darcy crushed her to him once again. "I am glad. So very glad."

"Fitzwilliam, we are on the street."

"I do not care," Darcy replied.

"You must meet Sally."

Darcy slowly released Elizabeth from his embrace but took one of her hands in his. He would keep her at his side and safe until she was once again within the wall of Darcy House.

"Mr. Darcy," the lady from the doorway had descended the steps.

"Sally?" he inquired.

The older woman smirked. "That is what they call me."

"But that is not her name," he heard Lydia whisper to Richard, who, Darcy noticed, had his arm protectively around Lydia's shoulder as Lydia held Dash. He had to admit in that moment and in the limited light of the lamp and what spilled from the house behind them, Richard and Lydia looked very well-together, perfectly at ease, as if they belonged as they were now.

"Not many know my given name," the woman

replied with a laugh. "Come. You may tell your gentlemen your story in my sitting room." She raised a brow at Elizabeth who had just opened her mouth to say something. "It is better to share it there than on the street where anyone who passes or drives a carriage might hear it."

She turned to her footman, who was standing next to the carriage. "Have the driver stay in case he is still needed, remind him that he only gets called because of his discretion, and see to the gentlemen's horses. We will not be long, but I should hate for them to wander off."

The footman nodded, and Sally turned back to lead the group to her sitting room. Once they were in her private quarters and seated, she looked at Miss Lydia. "You might as well begin. I do think you were telling me that this whole adventure was your doing."

Lydia bit her lip and looked from Richard to Darcy and back. "I did not intend for it to be," she began. Then, much to Darcy's surprise, the always bold Lydia Bennet dissolved into tears.

Elizabeth moved to go to her sister, but Darcy held her beside him. Richard could deal with a few tears. Indeed, he seemed to be doing a fine job of soothing Lydia.

"I am sorry," Lydia sobbed into Dash's neck.

Darcy was reminded of another young girl sobbing after being tricked by Wickham, and compassion for Lydia washed over him. He waited a moment until, under Richard's soothing caresses of her back and whispered reassurances, she calmed.

"I will not dismiss any guilt you may hold in this ordeal," Darcy began, "however, both my cousin and I know how artful Wickham can be."

"You do?" Lydia sniffled and peeked up at him, fear and question mingled in her eyes.

Darcy nodded and smiled. He had seen that look before as well. It was a look of a young lady seeking his approval and hoping she had not lost his good opinion. It was something he expected from Georgiana but seeing Lydia Bennet longing for his approval was unexpected.

"You are not the first young woman to need rescuing from him," he replied softly.

"Dash gave us this," Richard said, taking Wickham's letter from his pocket.

"I was not going to go with him. I only went to

tell him I could not marry him because I did not love him." She shrugged, and her lips trembled. "I did not know he would not take us home."

Richard placed his arm around her shoulder and drew her to his side. "He has been rewarded for his lack of care for you both. I dare say he'll not trouble you again."

"What did you do?" Lydia's eyes were wide.

"We pummelled him," Richard replied bluntly. "And Dash growled and barked at him."

Lydia's eye turned from Richard to Darcy.

"You hit him, too?"

Darcy nodded. "Several times."

Lydia blinked. "I did not think you knew how."

Richard threw his head back and laughed loudly.

"I may not do it so often as my cousin," Darcy replied with a glare for Richard, "but when you have a cousin such as Richard, you must learn how to fight."

Lydia blinked again. "I had not thought of that. Did you spend a lot of time together when you were young?"

"Lydia, could we focus on the matter at hand," Elizabeth inserted.

Lydia scowled. "I'd rather not."

Darcy chuckled.

"But we must," Elizabeth replied.

Lydia sighed. "Very well. We got into his carriage. I told him I could not go to Scotland with him. He said some rude things and told us to get out." She lifted her chin. "He did not like it at all that Lizzy likes Mr. Darcy or that I preferred a colonel to a lieutenant."

Darcy saw a look of pure horror wash over Lydia's face as she realized what she had said.

"Do you?" Richard asked with a chuckle.

Lydia's cheeks glowed rosy, but she lifted her chin. "Who would not?" she said without looking at him. "And then we walked here. I made a man give me a shilling for a kiss because he would not let us enter without kissing him, and Lizzy refused. And then we met Sally."

"You did what?" Richard interrupted the stream of words flowing forth from Lydia as quickly as water from an upturned pot.

"I met Sally," Lydia replied.

"Before that." There was a slight growl in Richard's tone.

Lydia huffed. "There was this gentleman who would not let us enter without giving him a kiss.

So, I told him I would kiss one cheek for a shilling or both cheeks for a half-crown. He gave me a shilling, so I grabbed his nose," she demonstrated on her own nose turning her head away from Richard as she did, "and pinched it while giving him a kiss on the cheek."

"You grabbed his nose?"

"Of course. I did not want him to turn his head. Our agreement was only for a kiss on the cheek. Nowhere else. And then we met Sally."

"And we had tea, and I found some clothes for them to wear to their uncle Gardiner's." Sally shook her head. "To think I met Fanny Gardiner's girls," she muttered. This, of course, led to a relating once again of the tale of how Mr. Bennet rescued Mrs. Bennet at Sally's house.

A quarter hour later, as Darcy handed Elizabeth into the hackney and waited for Lydia and Dash to be settled inside, he thanked the Lord for directing Mrs. Bennet to this house twenty some years ago, and then guiding Elizabeth and Lydia to the same place tonight.

He turned and looked at Richard as the carriage began to move, and they waited to follow it to Darcy House.

Richard nodded. "I feel exceptionally grateful to have met Mrs. Bennet."

"Who would have thought?" Darcy muttered, a smile spreading across his face.

Chapter 29

Abrams greeted the returning party at the door to Darcy House.

"How is everyone?" Darcy inquired as he handed his hat and coat to his butler.

"There has been much pacing of the hall from Mr. Bennet's room to Miss Georgiana's and back. I was nearly required to call the physician to inquire after his opinion about whether Mr. Bennet could be moved, but Miss Bennet calmed her mother."

Darcy sighed as he tucked Elizabeth's hand into the crook of his arm. "I can only imagine the worry she must have faced." He shook his head. "Two daughters lost to the night is no small thing."

"It is understandable, sir. We are all happy to see everyone returned safely."

"Oh, Mr. Darcy!" Mrs. Bennet stood at the top of

the stairs. "Have you found them?" She waved her handkerchief as she began to descend to them.

"We will come up to you," Darcy replied. "Both Elizabeth and Lydia are well."

"You are too good, sir. Too good."

Jane wrapped an arm around her mother's shoulders and moved her down the hall.

"Mr. Bennet's room," Darcy called to her. "Your father will wish to know the full story," he added to Elizabeth.

"He will not rest until he does," she agreed.

"What troubles you?"

Elizabeth's brow was furrowed with grief.

"The distress we have caused." She shrugged one shoulder. "I knew that our being gone would cause worry, but I am afraid in my focus on seeing us safe, I had forgotten about the anguish Mama would feel."

"Your focus was just as it ought to have been," he replied as they mounted the stairs behind Dash. He stepped to the side to allow Richard and Lydia to chase after the escaped pup.

"Your mother was in good hands." He blew out a breath. "We must tell her of our betrothal."

Elizabeth laughed. "If we do not, Lydia will."

"You told Lydia?"

Elizabeth nodded. "It seemed right."

Her head tipped, and he knew she was thinking about something, so he said nothing, choosing to wait to hear her thoughts. They climbed three steps before she spoke.

"Lydia's visit to Darcy House has been good for her. Even our ordeal tonight, though I would not wish it on anyone, was to her benefit." She sighed. "And your cousin and your dog seem to be the reason. She is beginning to think not as a girl but as a young woman. That is why I told her. She seemed to finally understand the solemnity of marriage, but I do not trust her to keep it a secret. She tends to speak before she thinks, much like my mother." She shook her head and laughed lightly. "I do not think that is a lack of maturity but rather just part and parcel of who they are."

"We comes to view others differently when we pause to consider them through a different lens," Darcy said.

They had reached the top of the stairs. There was not a great deal of corridor to traverse before they reached Mr. Bennet's room, and they could only saunter so slowly. Therefore, Darcy spoke quickly to clarify his statement.

"I have come to understand better your sisters and your mother – even your father. Though I would not wish an injury on anyone, your father's fall has been a blessing. I do not know where else I would have been given such opportunities to be intimately acquainted with you or your family." He shook his head at her attempted protest. "In Hertfordshire, I would be at Netherfield, and you would be three miles away. We would not pass hours sitting across a chessboard, hearing tales of the past or sharing banter over breakfast. Nor would we see one another in passing as we retired for the night or rose to face the day." He covered Elizabeth's hand, which lay on his arm with his free hand. "I like her – them. I am pleased to be adding them to my family."

"Truly," he added in response to her shocked expression. "They may still be trying at times, but it is far easier to overlook a few eccentricities in those we care for than it is in strangers."

"Do you mean it?" She blinked her eyes, which were glistening with tears.

"I do." He lifted her hand and kissed her fingers.

Then with a nod toward the open door, he whispered, "Are you ready to go delight your mother with the news of our betrothal?" He winked. "After Lydia finishes regaling them with her tale of adventure, that is."

Lydia's voice could be heard telling her mother about how detestable Mr. Wickham was, and Dash was adding his agreement with an occasional bark.

Elizabeth's expression did not say she was ready, but she nodded.

He lifted her fingers and kissed them once more before leading her into the room.

"Sally?" Mrs. Bennet squeaked as they entered the room.

"Yes, Mama. She knew you," Lydia said.

"Sally?" Mrs. Bennet repeated as she fanned her face.

"They were fortunate enough to stumble upon someone who knew you," Darcy inserted. "I must thank you for having met her those years ago, for it was the memory of you and Mr. Bennet which led her to take particularly fine care of your daughters."

"Was it a brothel?" Mary asked.

"Mary!" Jane scolded.

"Yes," Richard replied.

"And someone knew Mama there?" Mary continued to question, ignoring her sister's second scold.

Lydia did not waste a moment in sharing a well-crafted tale of a damsel in distress being rescued first by a kind woman and then a handsome gentleman.

"And that has something to do with that horrid Mrs. Salter?" Mary inquired.

"Yes, there is something there," Mrs. Bennet replied softly, carefully inspecting the hem on her handkerchief.

"And you met her how long ago?"

Miss Mary was not one to just hope to discover details. She seemed to be the sort that actively sought them even if the questions were at times somewhat awkward. Darcy attributed it to a keen mine and an ample supply of her father's inquisitiveness.

"More than twenty years ago!" Lydia's tone was slightly exasperated as if it was not necessary for Mary to have asked such an obvious question.

Mary's brows furrowed, and her lips pressed together as she shrugged. "It is very like Joseph; do you not think? His brothers meant to be rid of him, but God had a different purpose."

"Oh, Mary!" Mrs. Bennet scolded. "Now is not the time for sermons! Indeed, I am not sure when it is the time for a young lady to moralize as you do."

Mary scowled but held her peace.

"She is right, Mama," Kitty said softly. "Your horrible ordeal did provide a blessing just as Mr. Darcy said."

"I would rather not speak of that ordeal," Mrs. Bennet said sternly and then shrugged, "though I am happy it helped my daughters."

"You have always said you would do anything for us, Mama," Elizabeth said with an impertinent grin.

"Elizabeth!" Mrs. Bennet cried.

"Oh!" Lydia's eyes grew wide, and her hand flew to cover her mouth as she looked at Elizabeth.

"What is it?" Mrs. Bennet asked.

Lydia shook her head.

Elizabeth smiled at her. "You may share it."

"Truly? I may tell Mama?"

"Yes," Elizabeth replied.

"Lizzy is getting married," Lydia declared, "to Mr. Darcy."

"Is it true?" Georgiana asked her brother from where she sat next to Kitty.

Darcy nodded.

Mrs. Bennet squealed in delight and jumped from her chair to kiss Elizabeth on the cheek.

"Oh, Mr. Darcy," she said, "you are too good." She turned to Mr. Bennet. "You knew and did not tell me?"

He chuckled. "Your daughter wished to tell you in the morning."

"She does like to vex me," Mrs. Bennet muttered as she took her seat again. The smile she wore spoke loudly of the fact that such a vexation was more a delight than a torment. "We shall have to go shopping. Jane and Lizzy both need wedding clothes."

And with that statement, the ordeal of the night seemed to be over, and the future seemed all important.

"Not today, of course. We shall sleep today and do some quiet activities. And I shall write to your aunt with the news." Her brows furrowed. "We should visit her tomorrow. She will surely know all the best places to procure what we need." Mrs. Bennet rose. "Mary, Kitty, Lydia, it is time for bed."

"I should like to speak with my youngest daughter," Mr. Bennet interjected.

"She has had a trying night, my dear," Mrs. Bennet replied.

"As have we all," her husband said.

Mrs. Bennet pulled herself a little straighter and looked at Lydia. "You heard your father, Lydia. Mary, Kitty, come."

"My good woman," Mr. Bennet called, raising an eyebrow when she turned toward him. "I require a proper parting."

Mrs. Bennet looked around the room uneasily.

"They shall all avert their eyes," Mr. Bennet commanded.

"We shall leave you to your peace," Darcy said with a chuckle. "Do you require Elizabeth?"

Mr. Bennet shook his head. "I should like to hear her thoughts tomorrow, and those of you and the colonel, but I do not require that tonight." He looked at Lydia. "See that Dash is in his proper place and return."

"Yes, Papa," Lydia followed Elizabeth out of the room. "He loves Mama very much."

"He does," Elizabeth agreed.

"And he is very angry with me."

"Is he not right to be?" Richard asked.

Lydia's gaze dropped to the floor as she nodded.

"Come along. Let's see that pup to his bed," Richard held out his arm to her. "He was very worried about you..." His voice faded as he moved away from Darcy.

"I should like a proper parting as well," Darcy whispered to Elizabeth.

Elizabeth looked down the hall. Nearly everyone had disappeared inside a room.

"Very well, Mr. Darcy, but if my mother sees us..."

"I will take full responsibility," he muttered, pulling her into his embrace and kissing her as he had wanted to do from the moment he saw she was safe.

Chapter 30

"Ah, Mr. Bennet!" Bingley said as he entered the sitting room at Darcy House two days later. "I see the physician is pleased enough with your improvement to allow you to leave your bed."

"Happily. Yes," Mr. Bennet replied. "Although I cannot rise to greet you."

"I am just pleased to see you in the sitting room," Bingley replied.

"Papa's improvement means we will be returning home soon," Jane said as Bingley took a seat next to her.

"Not until all the lace in London has been purchased," Mr. Bennet said with a laugh.

"Everything will be ordered or purchased by the beginning of the week," Elizabeth inserted. "Mama is very efficient at seeing a plan put into action."

For the past two days, Elizabeth and Jane had

been required to follow their mother from their aunt's house to their uncle's warehouse and then to a variety of shops. Gloves, hats, dresses, slippers, whatever Mrs. Bennet thought a new young wife of a wealthy gentleman might require — and Mrs. Gardiner agreed was a necessity — had been listed out and attended to.

Lydia had wished to go with them on their excursions, but Mr. Bennet had required her to sit with him for a portion of each day – the same portion of the day in which her mother would be shopping.

There would be fittings and such in Meryton, but whatever could be acquired in London to quicken the preparations had been purchased.

"I have sent a letter to Mrs. Nichols just this morning," Bingley replied. "Everything at Netherfield should be ready for our arrival. Will you be joining us, Colonel?"

Richard had just stepped into the sitting room.

"I've not seen you in your uniform in days," Darcy commented. Between the uniform and the grave expression Richard wore, Darcy knew that the news his cousin bore was not good.

"I am to be in Manchester by next week," he said

simply. "I am to leave immediately." He held up a missive. "There is no time to waste."

"Leaving?" Lydia cried. "Now?"

Richard nodded. "There have been reports of fires and attacks on mills in the north, and the government expects it to only increase. There is a bill..." He sighed and then forced a smile. "This is my profession."

"Will you return?" Lydia was blinking rapidly, yet despite her best efforts, Darcy saw a tear slide down her cheek.

"Eventually."

"You must come to Netherfield when you do," Bingley offered.

"Yes," Lydia agreed. There was a hint of desperation in the word.

"And call at Longbourn," Mr. Bennet added.

"I would like that very much," Richard replied. "If all goes well, perhaps my journey will not be too long in duration, but with the sanctions that are coming..."

Darcy rose from his chair. "It will not be a pleasant affair."

"It never is a pleasant affair when I am sent to see

to it." Richard's attempt at a chuckle was weak. "I will write when I am settled."

"I'd not be opposed to a letter reaching Longbourn." Mr. Bennet shrugged when Richard turned his direction. "My wife and certain of my daughters will worry."

Richard paused.

Darcy could see the indecision on his face. Then, after a quick glance at Lydia, Richard's expression shifted to a look with which Darcy was more familiar — that of a colonel with a mission before him that must be fulfilled.

"Might I send it to Miss Lydia?" Richard asked.

Darcy smiled at the declaration of Richard's intent. It was like him to come directly to the point when a decision had been made. Richard was not one to dance around an issue, and Darcy was glad for it. For Richard to have gone off to Manchester without making his attachment known, or worse — denying it, would have made a miserable job that much more unbearable.

"Do you know what you ask?" Mr. Bennet replied.

"I do."

Darcy's gaze shifted from his cousin to Lydia,

who was likely holding her breath from the way in which she was sitting so motionless.

"And what of your family? We are not of your sphere and should things progress favourably, Lydia has little by way of fortune."

Lydia's expression fell, and Darcy turned his observation back to Richard.

"I have considered that, sir, and I cannot say with any certainty what will transpire at such a juncture. All I can promise is that I do not seek such a privileged acquaintance with your daughter without thought, and I am prepared to endure whatever censure may arise."

Darcy had never seen his cousin shift so uncomfortably, but then, his cousin had never, to this point, lost his heart. And from the reluctance with which Richard seemed to be reporting for his duty to the crown – the profession to which he had proclaimed himself happily married – Darcy knew that Richard was more than a little attached to Lydia. He had finally found a reason to leave his life of single devotion to his commission behind.

It still surprised Darcy that it was not some lady of the ton with a fortune as beautiful as her face but rather a simple country miss, who was not always sensible, who had wrought such a change. However, Darcy could not deny the fact that the Bennet ladies held a certain power that no sense of duty or demand of relations could quench.

His eyes shifted to Mr. Bennet. That was likely how a man as seemingly astute as Mr. Bennet had gained a wife so unlike him. His lips tipped up on one side as he considered that perhaps that was why the man knew he did not need a fortune for his daughters. They had inherited something far more valuable than tuppence and crowns from their mother.

Mr. Bennet nodded slowly and then turned to his youngest daughter. "Lydia, would you welcome a letter from the colonel?"

Lydia's head bobbed up and down rapidly, and she smiled through her tears. "Very much, Papa."

"Then I suggest you see the gentleman to his horse and make certain he knows the direction to put on the envelope." He turned back to Richard. "I wish you well on your journey. May you return to us safely."

"Thank you, sir." Richard turned to Darcy. "I will write."

"Take care," Darcy replied. He disliked these

times when he had to part with his cousin and friend, not knowing if the man would return to him or not.

"I saw Georgie upstairs," Richard said.

"Is she well?"

"No, but she assures me she will be." He stooped to scruff the top of Dash's head. "I shall miss you. Keep my chair warm." Then with a final word of parting for each of the others in the room, he departed with Lydia at his side.

"He will be well," Elizabeth whispered as she came to stand next to Darcy.

Darcy was unsure if she said it to reassure him or herself. Either way, he was thankful for it. It would be a trifle easier to endure this separation with her presence to cheer and distract him.

"Walk with me?" he asked.

"Of course." Elizabeth took his arm. "Are you well?" she asked as they walked down the hall to his study.

Apparently, she had made her comment, at least in part, to reassure him. He nodded his reply but said nothing until they were inside the study.

"I will not lie. I worry about him every time he leaves." He pulled her into his embrace. "But I think I can endure it far better this time with you by my side." He kissed her forehead.

They stood silently for a moment, her head against his chest, arms wrapped around each other as they did nothing but breath and be.

"He's never courted anyone before," Darcy finally voiced a portion of the thoughts swirling in his mind. "He's never even hinted at wishing to court someone before."

"Lydia has attempted to draw several gentlemen along enough to court her," Elizabeth replied with a small laugh.

"They are very different from each other, are they not?" Darcy looked down at Elizabeth and smiled.

"They are," she replied.

"And yet they seem to fit well together."

Elizabeth's cheek rubbed against his jacket as she nodded her agreement.

"Just as we do." He pulled back far enough so that he could look at those captivating eyes of hers which spoke to him even when she didn't say a word. At this moment, they were speaking of happiness and contentment – or was that just his heart reflecting itself in her eyes? Whichever it was, he did not care. "I love you, Elizabeth."

She smiled. "And I love you, Fitzwilliam."

He kissed her once, just lightly, and was about to speak again when he thought better of it and kissed her again. This time he kissed her deeply, and for some minutes. Finally, when his mind was wandering to wishes beyond kisses, and his hands were itching to roam, he leaned his forehead against hers.

"I have spoken to my uncle about our betrothal." This was not news to her, he had told her he was going to visit the earl. "And I stressed that now was not a good time to visit as your father is still recovering."

"Are you afraid to have them meet my family?"

He smiled at her playful tone. "Perhaps," he teased and then shook his head. "His schedule is busy at present. There was no need to push things aside for us. There will be plenty of years for them to get to know you and your family. He gave me his blessing without more than a question or two about who you were. I believe he is just happy that I am finally marrying. Of course, that was my uncle. His sister, my aunt Catherine will be less obliging."

"She is the one with the daughter to whom you are *not* betrothed?"

She was teasing him again, and willingly, he played along.

"Yes, she is that as well as your cousin's *esteemed* patroness."

They both chuckled.

Darcy wrapped her tightly in his embrace one more time before giving her another quick kiss and releasing her.

"We should return to the others, no matter how much I wish to just remain here with you."

She wrapped her arm around his and leaned her head against his shoulder as they walked back toward the sitting room. "It is not many days until we are in Hertfordshire. Do you think you can continue to tolerate my family even in the wilds surrounding Netherfield?"

"I believe I am up to the challenge," he replied with a chuckle.

"My mother will be delighted to have you and Mr. Bingley to reintroduce to the neighbourhood. Are you prepared for that?"

Darcy looked down at her upturned, smiling face. "I believe I can endure anything for you."

"Even Sir William and my aunt Philips?"

"Have I not yet proven myself enough to you?"

She shrugged and pursed her lips as she tried to contain her smile. However, she could do nothing to hide the sparkle of amusement in her eyes.

"Just you wait and see, Elizabeth," he said, pitching his voice low. "I shall perform admirably."

She giggled. "I do not doubt you will."

"Yet you question me most severely." He darted a look up and down the corridor before giving her impertinent, puckered lips a quick kiss.

"Mr. Darcy!"

Had she not been smiling, her scold might have given him a moment of pause. However, she was smiling, so he kissed her again. "That, my dear, is my promise."

"Your promise of what?"

He took both her hands in his and grew serious. "It is my promise that come what may, I shall endure it all, for I love you – and that is a fact which I will not allow you to forget."

"You will not?" Delight shone in her eyes.

He shook his head. "And do you know how I will remind you?"

Her left eyebrow arched. "How?"

He lifted her hands. "By kissing you." He kissed the knuckles of both her right and left hands, and then, leaning forward, he pressed his lips against hers one final time before returning with her to the sitting room where a very delighted Mrs. Bennet was presiding over a discussion of wedding breakfast receipts.

Darcy knew that his life would never be without some amount of liveliness and possible chaos, thanks to his new family. However, the thought of it did not unsettle him as it once might have. Instead, he welcomed it – not with eager anticipation, but with calm assurance. As he had told Elizabeth, he was determined to endure it all, for he could not, would not, face life without her by his side, no matter what might lie ahead.

Before You Go

If you enjoyed this book, be sure to let others know by leaving a review.

~*~*~

Want to know when other books in this series will be available?

You can always know what's new with my books by subscribing to my mailing list.

(There will, of course, be a thank you gift for joining because I think my readers are awesome!)

Book News from Leenie Brown

(http://eepurl.com/bSɪeIɪ)

~*~*~

Turn the page to read an excerpt of *Loving Lydia*, book three in the *Marrying Elizabeth Series*

Loving Lydia Excerpt

As I mentioned in the note at the beginning of this book, Delighting Mrs. Bennet was first posted as a work in progress on my website each Thursday. The next book in this series is posting there now. Loving Lydia is still a work in progress and will not be published for some time, but if you wish, you can follow along as I write the book at this link, which will take you to the Thursday's Three Hundred section of leeniebrown.com.

Below, is the first chapter as it appears on my website.

Chapter 1

"Are you certain you will be well?" Fitzwilliam Darcy asked his sister, Georgiana. They had just arrived at Netherfield, and she was still getting settled into her room while he leaned against the doorframe, watching.

Dash sniffed his way around the perimeter of the room. Why Darcy had allowed himself to be talked into bringing that dog by three young ladies, he was not certain. It was likely his inability to say no to three sets of begging eyes. He shook his head. He was becoming soft – dreadfully soft. He reached down and scratched Dash's ear when he came to sniff Darcy's boots for the third time.

"I am certain I will survive if I have to see him. I am not without friends or you." She turned and looked at him while she held her jewelry box. She always saw to the arranging of her dressing table. "I am not as foolish as I once was. I do not trust him, and I know for a fact that Miss Lydia and Miss Kitty no longer like him either. You have very little to fear."

"I will worry nonetheless."

She smiled. "Of course, you will. You are most proficient at worrying about me."

It was true. He did excel at worrying about many things – his sister had been at the top of that list, followed by his cousin Colonel Richard Fitzwilliam. However, Georgiana would now find that top position a trifle crowded, for there was now Elizabeth and her sisters – most especially Miss Lydia – about whom to worry.

"There." Georgiana stepped back and admired

her table. "Everything is just as it should be." She glanced around the room. "Where is Dash?"

Darcy sighed and pushed off the doorframe. "He must have escaped."

"Which is not hard to do when the door is standing open."

"You have grown a tad impertinent over the past few weeks."

"And your smile says you are not truly displeased."

He offered her his arm when she exited her room.

"I cannot say that I am as long as your impertinence keeps its place."

"Which is not in public," Georgiana replied.

"Precisely."

"What is the cause of that sigh?"

Darcy grimaced. He had not meant to sigh, but thoughts of impertinence and worry naturally turned his mind to Lydia Bennet. "I was remembering my promise to Richard."

"What promise is that?"

"I am not certain I should say."

"Is it that dreadful?" Her tone was teasingly horrified.

He chuckled. "That depends on how you receive the information. I know Miss Lydia is your friend."

"Please? I know he loves her and that he has asked for permission to write to her while he is away."

Darcy nodded. That was all true. But how did he explain the rest? "This might be said badly," he cautioned. "Richard asked me to help Miss Lydia improve."

"Improve what?" Her brow was furrowed as she attempted to understand his meaning.

"Her behaviour in public is not precisely how it should be."

"Oh! I had not considered it, but I do see what you mean. She does speak more freely than I was taught to do."

"And her choices of topics are not always the best – such as asking you if you had a beau at your first meeting."

Georgiana nodded her head. "I understand. It could put her in a place to be ridiculed and hurt. Richard would never wish for that."

"Indeed, he would not." It impressed him how Georgiana had so succinctly stated what the jumbled mess of thoughts in his mind seemed unable to tell him clearly. "I could not have said it better. That is it precisely."

Georgiana patted his arm. "Then we have nothing to fear. I shall behave properly as I usually do, and Mrs. Annesley can assist us. I shall have her spend some time teaching me things that I already know, but that Miss Lydia and Miss Kitty might not know."

It seemed as if it was a plan which might work, but... "I do not wish to tax Mrs. Annesley too much."

"I will ask her, and if she so much as hesitates in replying, I will think of another plan that shall be just as good."

Darcy grimaced as he heard a crash in the drawing room. "I think we have found Dash."

As suspected, Dash was in the drawing room next to a vase which lay in pieces on the floor.

"It was not him," Bingley said in response to Darcy's growled *Dash*. "Did I tell you I acquired a kitten for Miss Bennet?"

Darcy blinked and looked at Bingley. "You did what?"

"Before I left town, Miss Bennet was telling me about a cat she once had but which ran away during a storm. She seemed to miss it a great deal, so when I arrived, I sought out Sir William and inquired if he knew where I might find a grey tabby cat. As luck would have it, he knew precisely where I might find one." Bingley lifted the drapes out of the way and scooped up a kitten. "This is Oliver. He has yet to learn not to push vases off tables."

Bingley crossed the room to where Dash sat. "Dash this is Oliver," he said crouching down.

When Dash sniffed the creature, Oliver meowed and attempted to climb Bingley's arm.

"He is a friend," Bingley scolded.

"You are talking to a cat as if he can understand you," Darcy said flatly.

"Who is to say he cannot," Bingley returned. "I think it would be best if they become friends."

"This is what you were doing for two days before we arrived? Acquiring a kitten."

Bingley released Oliver who looked at Dash for only a moment before returning to his hiding spot behind the drapery.

"No, no, I was also making certain all was ready for your arrival." He blew out a breath. "And that of my sister. She arrives tomorrow."

"Sir Matthew will be joining her?"

Bingley nodded. "Thankfully. No, Oliver. He is a friend."

"Perhaps Dash should be made comfortable in your room," Darcy suggested.

Dash had gone to attempt to make friends with Oliver, but Oliver was none too complacent about the whole idea and had decided it would be best to climb to safety.

"This might not have been my best idea," Bingley said with a laugh as he tried to extricate Oliver's sharp claws from the fabric of the drapes.

"I am certain Miss Bennet will appreciate the gesture," Darcy assured him. He sighed. "I brought Dash for Georgiana and Miss Lydia." He shrugged when Bingley looked at him. "I found it impossible to not grant their request."

Bingley laughed. "What has become of us?"

Darcy took a seat next to his friend. "We have found love, my friend, and it seems love addles one's brain."

Bingley shook his head. "No, our brains are not addled. We are just willing to do that which we might not otherwise do to see those we love happy."

"You do surprise me with your occasional astuteness," Darcy teased.

"I am impressive, am I not? If only Richard were here to tell me I was not."

Darcy sighed and nodded. How he wished the same! And not just because then Richard could worry about Miss Lydia. Nor did he wish it just to have Richard here to tease and taunt. He wished it because then he knew his cousin would be safe and not in harm's way. "I suspect I will receive some news of him soon, letting me know he has arrived in Manchester. That frame breaking bill will surely stir up more strife than it is intended to squelch."

"I cannot say I blame the frame breakers for their anger. I have witnessed some very grim living arrangements. However, as the son of a manufacturer, I cannot condone their actions either."

Both men sat in silence for some time. Darcy tapped his fingers on the arm of his chair, while Bingley ran his hand along Oliver's back, who was sleeping on his lap.

"I am sure he will be well," Bingley said, at last, putting into words what both were contemplating.

"He has survived worse," Darcy agreed. While he disliked the idea of Richard being in harm's way at all, he knew it was part and parcel of being a colonel in His Majesty's Forces. And, to Darcy's mind, it was better for Richard to be here in England rather than in France, where he had been in the past. While there might be some skirmishes in the North, they were unlikely to be as deadly as a battle on the continent.

Bingley rose from his chair with Oliver tucked in the crook of his arm. "I had planned on calling at Longbourn today for a few minutes. Will you and Georgiana be joining me?"

Darcy smiled. "Without a doubt." It had been nearly a full day since he had seen Elizabeth, and there was only so long a gentleman could go without seeing the lady he loved when he was used to having her under his roof where he could see her at all hours of the day. He was not sure how he was going to survive three miles of separation.

His eyes narrowed as he looked at Bingley. "Do you suppose Oliver could cause some calamity that would require both Miss Bennet and Miss Elizabeth to take up residence here?"

Bingley chuckled. "I do not think I am that clever."

Darcy sighed. "Neither am I, unfortunately, so I

suppose, I will have to do as regular gentlemen do and call on her at home."

Acknowledgements

There are many who have had a part in the creation of this story. Some have read and commented on it. Some have proofread for grammatical errors and plot holes. Others have not even read the story and a few, I know, will never read it. However, their encouragement and belief in my ability, as well as their patience when I became cranky or when supper was late or the groceries ran low, was invaluable.

And so, I would like to say *thank you* to Zoe, Rose, Betty, Kristine, Ben, and Kyle as well as my patrons on Patreon and the readers who faithfully read all those Thursday posts on my blog. I feel blessed by your help, support, and understanding.

I have not listed my dear husband in the above group because, to me, he deserves his own special thank you, for, without his somewhat pushy insistence that I start sharing my writing, none of my writing goals and dreams would have been met.

~*~*~

For those who might be interested in some of the inspiration and research links I used while writing this book — such as a picture of an adorable puppy, links to a few articles about the Frame Breaker's Act, which is not named but referred to in this story, or a link to a video of the cotillion danced under Mr. Hughes's exuberant instruction — I have a Pinterest board of those items and more at this link.

Other Leenie B Books

You can find all of Leenie's books at this link
[www.books2read.com/ap/8pOrNn/Leenie-Brown]
or choose to explore the collections below

~*~

Other Pens, Mansfield Park

~*~

Touches of Austen Collection

~*~

Other Pens, Pride and Prejudice

~*~

Dash of Darcy and Companions Collection

~*~

Marrying Elizabeth Series

~*~

Willow Hall Romances

DELIGHTING MRS. BENNET

~*~

The Choices Series

~*~

Darcy Family Holidays

~*~

Other Novels ~ Novellas ~ Shorts

About the Author

Leenie Brown has always been a girl with an active imagination, which, while growing up, was both an asset, providing many hours of fun as she played out stories, and a liability, when her older sister and aunt would tell her frightening tales. At one time, they had her convinced Dracula lived in the trunk at the end of the bed she slept in when visiting her grandparents!

Although it has been years since she cowered in her bed in her grandparents' basement, she still has an imagination which occasionally runs away with her, and she feeds it now as she did then — by reading!

Her heroes, when growing up, were authors, and the worlds they painted with words were (and still are) her favourite playgrounds! Now, as an adult, she spends much of her time in the Regency world, playing with the characters from her favourite Jane Austen novels and those of her own creation.

When she is not traipsing down a trail in an attempt to keep up with her imagination, Leenie resides in the beautiful province of Nova Scotia with her two sons and her very own Mr. Brown (a wonderful mix of all the best of Darcy, Bingley, and Edmund with a healthy dose of the teasing Mr. Tilney and just a dash of the scolding Mr. Knightley).

Connect with Leenie

E-mail:
LeenieBrownAuthor@gmail.com
Facebook:
www.facebook.com/LeenieBrownAuthor
Blog:
leeniebrown.com
Patreon:
https://www.patreon.com/LeenieBrown
Subscribe to Leenie's Mailing List:
Book News from Leenie Brown
(http://eepurl.com/bSɪeIɪ)
Join Leenie on Austen Authors:
austenauthors.net